CHOTI MAA

HARSH AGRAWAL

Made with ❤ on the Notion Press Platform
www.notionpress.com

Dedication

In the loving memory of my father Shri Rajkumar Agrawal. He was an obedient son and a loving father. He was always full of life, brave and had a helping & giving nature. Forever in my heart!

I Miss You....

I would also like to dedicate this book to my Mother Smt Mridul Agarwal and my "Isht Dev" Lord Krishna. I am nothing without their blessings. Lord Krishna is the original writer of this story; I am just a medium.

I bow down to you oh my Lord...

.... Take me under your protection and refuge.

Acknowledgements

Thanks to my father for being the inspiration behind this book. He is not there with us but will always be in our hearts.

Special thanks to my mother and father for instilling in me rich values the outcome of which is this story.

A heartfelt thanks to my wife for guiding me throughout the process of authoring this book. She has been a strong pillar of support for me and will always be indebted to her.

Foreword

I have known Harsh from 9 years. He has tried to highlight all our emotions that we have gone through our parenthood journey of twin girls through this book. It will give readers a glimpse about what exactly a parenthood is all about and what all a parent had to go through to raise a kid. He has really given it a distinctive touch by vividly explaining parent and a child relation.

It will make you feel connected with what our parents have done for us to make us a wonderful human being!!

The parenthood Journey is full of roller coaster sometimes it will make you feel on top of the world and on another it might be gloomy as well, but the overall experience I guarantee will make us a better person as a small one life depends upon us.

Hope readers will be able to connect with sea of emotions which he has tried to portrait.

Happy Reading!!

Ayushi Agarwal

Preface

It is quite common to see teenagers and young adults in the age group of 20-30 yrs to lose interest in parents and find happiness in friends and outside world. They start taking parents for granted. They just need parents to fund their lifestyle. They consider parents as a bad manager in a company to whom they must compulsorily report. Parents ignore the same thinking that its due to the age factor and will become better with time. It is a common phenomenon across the world. Youngsters do not realize how important parents are in their life. Even if they are self-dependent still parents are key to their existence. They will only realize it upon losing them.

Therefore, this book is an attempt to make them realize how important parents are at every step of life. It is an attempt to bring them closer to reality and bring them back from the glamorous and mean outside world. Hope this purpose is achieved and the readers feel the emotions that I have tried to convey.

Author –

Harsh Agrawal

Contents

Chapter 1

The Agrawal Family

It is a cloudy morning of August. It has rained last night, and some dark clouds are still looming around. Its drizzling for few seconds and stopping. This process gets repeated every 15 mins. For some its dull and gloomy and for others it is a pleasant climate. Streets are all wet with patches on the side of the road filled with water. Some enthusiastic people are still coming out for a morning walk even in this rainy climate. Small tea shop on the street have already opened in such early morning hours with customers waiting to enjoy a hot cup of tea in this cloudy weather. Newspaper boy is already doing rounds of the locality distributing the latest newspaper. One such newspaper enters the house of Agrawals also.

This Agrawal family is one of the rich families of the town having primary business of stock market trading and investment consultancy. Madhav Agrawal is the head of this family who started this venture. He is a very workaholic person who likes to spend most of the time in office. He is a truly knowledgeable person and speaks very less and to the point. He has a wife Radha who is a homemaker. She is a quite simple women with her world revolving around her family. She does not believe in socializing much. They have one teenage daughter named Sia.

They are expecting a new member in the family after a gap of fourteen long years. So naturally everyone is excited but anxious as well hoping for the best and praying for god's blessings. Overall, it is a small family of 3 (would be 4). As they had only one daughter till now, they pampered her a lot. This made her into a rich spoiled brat. Both the parents never fail to fulfil any of her demands. They wanted to give her best of everything but in the process, they ended up making her a selfish girl with absolutely no signs of humbleness.

Give a flavour of her personality, one day when she was getting ready for school, mom made some healthy sandwich and fruit juice for breakfast. However, Sia found the breakfast too boring and left the house empty stomach showering her irritation on mom and saying she will have something in school canteen. She did not even care looking at her mom while she screamed at her mom. All this while she was glued to her mobile chatting with her friends. She did not even show any concern for her mother who is already 8+ months pregnant and is still making breakfast for her which she could have done it for herself.

Even her father does not like this trait of Sia. He expects her to behave decently and have tried to explain it to her as well, but she does not listen. But still overall he is fond of her daughter being the first child. He trusts her with everything. She may have attitude but no doubt she is trustworthy not only for her parents but for everyone. Her father has told her everything like where he has kept cash money at home, what is the password of the safe, his bank ATM pin and what not. Whenever Sia demands for anything, her father does not give money to her instead he gives the entire wallet to her every single time. He never asks for her expenditure details as well. Apart from love for her daughter another reason for doing that is he knows that Sia is a very smart buyer, she bargains a lot and voluntary gives detailed explanation for each expense, and she will never even think of stealing. Whatever she wants she will ask and demand for it from her parents on their face but will never touch the money kept at home. That is why her father trusts her a lot.

Sia's parents never stopped her when she disrespected someone else or behaved selfish etc. They thought in this mean world it is fine to be like that for survival otherwise people will make use of her. Also, as she grows, she will learn by herself how to deal with the world and develop her own personality. Everyone has a distinctive style of parenting. This was theirs.

Chapter 2

Welcoming a New Member in the Family

Finally, the day has arrived when Radha has been taken to the hospital for delivery. Father is anxiously waiting outside the operation room along with his daughter Sia who does not seem to be interested at all. There are absolutely no signs of happiness, excitement in her. As always, she is sitting next to her father browsing her mobile phone. She fears that the undivided attention that she has been getting till now might end and parent's energy and love will shift towards the newborn. That is one of the reasons for her carelessness right now. She is not even excited about the fact that she will be having a sibling now. With an age gap of almost 14 yrs, she is in fact expected to take care of the baby like a second mother. However, she does not even care.

Madhav is feeling even more anxious as time passes by trying to hold her daughters' hand for some relaxation which is irritating her. The father who does everything for her, she does not even show basic courtesy to him also. She takes her father for granted. After a wait of an hour finally the doctor calls Madhav inside to introduce him to the newborn. As soon as Madhav enters the operation room, the doctor congratulates him and hands over the baby to him. It is a Boy – the doctor says in an excited voice. Madhav breaks into tears.

After all, they were blessed with a baby after 14 yrs. They underwent a lot of treatment to conceive a second child but met with failure every time. Only he knows the pain he went through in this entire process. With rising hopes at the start of every try, they would end up in despair every time due to some medical reason or the other. They lost all hope. It was then they took the spiritual route along with following what doctor said. They surrendered themselves to lord Hanuman and have been praying to him for the past couple of years following all rituals in proper Sanatana way making sure no mistakes happen. From keeping fasts, to offering prayers, donation, helping the needy etc, they did everything in their capacity to earn the blessings of lord Hanuman by doing good karma. It was not as if they were doing it just for their personal benefit. They believed in good karma and helping others right from the start. In addition to that Radha was following strict health routine including proper diet, yoga & meditation etc.

Today, God has blessed them and fulfilled their wish. Madhav still extremely high on emotions, immediately thanked lord Hanuman, chanted lord Rams name in the child's ear and hugged her wife. It was a magical moment of their life. They were living their dreams. Couple of days later, wife and the baby were discharged from hospital. All of them came back to their home, exuding uncontrollable happiness. This is all they wanted.

They started taking diligent care of the baby making all the necessary arrangements. Newborn parenting phase has begun. Feeding, cleaning, and playing with baby, sleepless nights are now common sight in the house. But the happiness overpowered every such pain.

They were just so happy except for Sia. She has already started feeling neglected and not able to digest this change. The duty of taking Sia's care has been transferred to the Maid. Earlier Mom used to do everything for Sia right from preparing breakfast, arranging school bag and everything. Now she has asked the old housekeeper to do it as she is too tied up.

This is making Sia even more furious. She expressed her anger on her parents saying that she is being neglected. Parents defended by saying that she should behave maturely and try to understand the situation and cooperate with them. They absolutely hated such behaviour from Sia specially in front of newborn as it might affect him. But they never said anything to her. They are considering it as a temporary phase in Sia's mind which will gradually fade away.

However as far as Sia is concerned she is getting furious day by day with no signs of improvement. She is mostly spending time outside with friends gossiping about her own brother and how he has made her life hell. By now all her friends are aware that Sia is not fond of her brother and in fact hates him. Most of her friends are finding it very odd as they thought Sia will be happy and excited. She could be seen just cribbing about her brother all the time to everyone she knows. Sia may regret this in future but currently she is enjoying doing it.

Chapter 3

Tragedy Strikes – Destiny had Another Plan

It has been approx. 3 months since the baby was born. He has been doing well except for minor traces of jaundice which is quite common these days with newborn kids. Doctor has asked the parents to expose the kid to some sunlight in the morning and give some vitamin D syrup and he shall be fine. No need for hospitalization.

One fine day as they all were busy playing with the kid in the living room, the Phone rings. They thought it will be someone ringing to congratulate them just like many other calls they have received. However, it was something else. A close friend of Madhav had suffered a heart stroke and was admitted to hospital. When he heard the news, he was shocked and really upset. He immediately wanted to meet his friend. Radha insisted to go as well as she was also remarkably close to his friend's wife. But they had a baby to look after and did not want to take the baby to the hospital to avoid any infection etc.

After much thought they decided that as the baby sleeps long hours so they can quickly visit their friend once the baby falls asleep, asking housekeeper and Sia to take care in their absence as they will be back within couple of hours. Their baby sleeps for 3 hours at a stretch, so they thought it is a fair idea and risk worth taking.

Next day, it was around 8 AM in the morning. The baby has a habit of getting up late in the morning by around 10:30-11 AM types. This was the best suited time to them considering the sleeping baby. They quickly got ready and took out the car. They reached hospital in around 30 mins and went to his friend's room. Friend was lying on the bed resting post operation. He is out of danger now. They spent some time with them, asked how it all happened and asked them to call anytime for any kind of help. All this while both were thinking about their son Raghav. Inside they were restless and wanted to leave as soon as possible. After spending some more time with them and giving the comfort which they deserve from a friend, they then asked permission from their friend to leave for home as baby might wake up anytime. The friend also understood their situation and allowed them to leave on a condition that they will visit again. They hugged each other and then left.

It is around 9:30 AM as they almost spent an hour in hospital. It is still foggy outside with low visibility. As Madhav drives cautiously in this foggy weather, he felt some object (a street dog) coming towards their car from the opposite direction. That object was not too far from their car and was approaching towards them quickly. He thought it can hit their car any moment so in order to save the object which he thought was most probably a street dog, he turned the steering towards left not knowing that the road repair work was going on that side with a large whole being dug to repair a pipe or something. The car immediately fell in the large hole from one side and turned upside down due to this imbalance. The car also hit one of the heavy machineries which was being used to dig the whole. It was a major collision making a loud noise that could be heard from far.

It was a major accident with both lying unconscious with blood flowing profusely. Quickly the nearby people came into action and tried to pull them out of the car. As the car tumbled upside down it was with great difficulty that they were brought out. Since there was construction work going on and lot of labourers were present at the site, at least there was no shortage of people to help. One of the labourers also got injured in the accident.

They were injured severely with blood stains all around. Someone called the ambulance, and they were all taken to the nearby hospital in the emergency section. Doctors immediately started attending them asking the person who brought them what has happened. This could help them diagnose better. Luckily, the labourer was not injured severely and was given stiches wherever required along with medicines. In case of Madhav and Radha, after cleaning the blood and performing the required tests, the doctors took them to the operation theatre to remove parts of machinery which had penetrated their body. There was severe blood loss and both were unconscious.

Nurses asked the person who brought them to find out the number of their relatives and call them up. The locals who brought them to hospital were able to get the number of their daughter Sia from Madhav's wallet and informed her about the incident. She was shocked to hear the news and started crying inconsolably. She asked the housekeeper to look after the kid and immediately rushed to the hospital. She reached the hospital, asked the way to the operation theatre, and ran towards it. She was asked to wait outside by the guard as the operation was in progress.

After a long operation of approx. 3-4 hours, doctors came out. Sia immediately rushed towards them and introduced herself. She then asked in a hurried way how are her parents. Doctor then told Sia that they are in Coma due to severe head injuries and blood loss. She burst into tears the very next second. The doctors tried to console her and asked her to wait patiently. They will give more updates in some time.

What happened to my parents, why did God do this to them, how will I live without them, all sorts of thoughts started popping up in her mind. Her heart filled with feelings of immense pain and sadness. She was inconsolable. She was not able to bear the pain. Never ever in her wildest dreams did she visualize such a scenario. Life has hit hard on her. There is absolutely no one to look after her and her newly born brother now. They do not have any relatives as her father was single child and so was her mother. Both the grand parents are no more.

At the least, she is aware of all her father's investments, savings, and insurance details so financially she is secured. She also knows how everything operates in banks, insurance companies etc as she was always curious about her father's profession and spent a lot of time with him understanding stuff. She completed all the necessary documentation of the hospital right from cashless insurance, various forms, and other formalities. There is nothing much she could do about her parents as of now apart from praying to God. It has already been 5 hrs now and the thought of her brother came to her mind - how was he, was he crying, is he hungry etc all sorts of questions started emerging in her mind. She checked with the doctors, and they asked her to go home as they will be keeping them under observation where Sia will not be permitted anyways so no point of her staying back.

She then left for home and on her way back she made some big decisions in her mind. She decided that, if anything happens to her parents, from now on she will take care of her brother, she will be her mother and will make sure he does not feel their absence at any cost. In just a moment she forgot all her hatred towards her brother. This is why it is important not to hold grudge against anyone as life is too short for all of this.

Trivia – That's why they say to be grateful, kind, and humble as life is too unpredictable and can teach a lesson in an extremely hard way if it wants.

Chapter 4

Learning Parenting

One week later, Sia had a detailed word with the senior doctor who is looking after the case of her parents. He told Sia that her parents are in Coma, but rest of their body parts are working fine. They cannot say when will they come back from coma if at all they come back. So, it is all on their will power and God's will now. They will be keeping her parents in a special room in the hospital under constant monitoring with a dedicated attendant. In case of any updates Sia will be informed immediately. The senior doctor gave his personal number to Sia and asked her to call him anytime.

Sia came home after this heavy conversation with the doctor. Though she was happy with the arrangements by the hospital and their professionalism, she was deeply disappointed from inside thinking about all that has happened. Her entire family is shattered. She now feels how dependant she was on her parents. All the while when they were there, she took them for granted. Now she misses them. If she would have been alone it was still manageable somehow but in front of her is her newly born brother. What will happen to him now. She who hated him for the past 3 months is now expected to take care of him like a parent. All her negativity regarding her brother suddenly vanished post her parents' accident. That event completely shook her and changed her beliefs.

She is now the sole decision maker of the house as she takes charge. She must take some strong and bold decisions now. Primarily, a decision about her own schooling. If she goes to school, then what will happen to the baby. Who will take care of him. She cannot trust the old housekeeper with the kid specially when she is away from home. Although she has been working in their house for years now, but Sia did not want to take any chances. There are no immediate relatives who can come to rescue in this crisis. It is a very isolated family with no uncle or aunts because for generations this family has had only single child and ironically her mother is also a single child. Overall Sia is on her own.

So, she decided to quit school as there did not seem to be any better option. Once her parents come back, she can rejoin. She drafted an email to the principal of the school informing about all that has happened and her inability to continue schooling. She then went and met the principal the next day and told her everything. The principal gave Sia exit from school with a heavy heart with an assurance that she can join back anytime once her parents are doing well.

Second major decision was regarding the old housekeeper. Should she keep her for helping in looking after the kid or shall she remove her as she might take advantage of the situation and involve in theft etc specially when there is only a teenage girl looking after the house. She then remembers that her mother used to say that she is very trustworthy and old age too. She does not have any family so does not have any high demands from life. She just wishes to continue working to keep herself busy and earn a living. Trusting her mother's words, she decides to keep her for now, so that she has a helping hand and experience from which to learn parenting. But she will make sure to keep an eye still just to ensure that there no changes in her intension post the incident.

She told the old housekeeper that she will be the primary person taking care of the child and she just needs to teach her all the aspects of parenting along with looking after rest of the household chores. Sia wanted the best for her brother as she was afraid of losing him also with parents already in coma. She would be left with no family in case anything happens to him and parents also do not come back. This thought scares the hell out of her. That is why she has become overly possessive of her brother suddenly in just a day. As if he is her son. This is a great start as far as positive change in Sia's attitude is concerned however tough journey lies ahead filled with unknown challenges.

Lesson 1 – So let the parenting begin!!

Milk pee lo - the first task that Sia starts with is feeding milk to the baby brother. She learnt how to prepare baby milk using the baby milk powder of the best brand in the town. She carefully warms water in an electric kettle, pours the water in the bottle with accurate measurement and mixed it with required portion of milk powder. Being her first time, it took her quite long to prepare the milk and the baby started crying. She rushes to pacify her brother by taking him in her arms and puts the bottle in his mouth. But parenting is not so straight forward. Due to this delay in preparing the milk, the baby has become cranky and is not accepting the milk. He is pushing the bottle, moving his mouth away from the bottle and spitting whatever milk entered his mouth. It can also be because it is an artificial milk and not her mother's natural milk which he is used to.

Initially Sia started getting irritated. Sometimes crying sound of the baby gets into your head. It triggers some part of your brain which immediately throws an intense sense of irritation and anger. In the moment, the person can end up doing any wild stuff like shouting, throwing stuff, getting physical etc. Thankfully in Sia's case it was not so extreme, and she was just intending to shout.

Watching the situation, the old housekeeper took the baby and started trying to calm him meanwhile Sia gathered herself. This reminds her of all the tantrums that she used to throw at her mother when she asked her to drink milk before leaving for school. How she used to make faces and sometimes even shout back at her mother for being so pushy. Many a times she used to leave home without finishing her milk or not even touching the glass. Now she understands how her mother would have felt. After all such tantrums, not even once did her mother shouted at her and always asked her politely to have milk. She is a very soft-hearted lady. It is now that Sia understands the beauty of her mother's sweet and caring nature and how such a disrespectful child she was.

She then controls her emotions, gathers herself and then gives another attempt at feeding her baby brother with all that warmth and love of her mother that she just recalled. She kept all her feelings of frustration and anger aside and decided to give her best shot just like her mother. And guess what, it worked. It always does. Nothing can beat a mother's warmth and care. The baby felt the love and comfort from his sister and accepted the milk. Sia has taken her first step towards parenting. It was quite an experience for her. Even such a basic activity of feeding milk taught her so much not only about parenting but about her own parents, her emotions, power of love and life overall.

Lesson 2 –
Sleepless night

Sia loves her sleep. She is so fond of sleeping that she can sleep 12 hrs at a stretch and can still feel sleepy throughout the rest of the day. It is her most favourite part of life – Sleeping. Less did she know that she is not going to get a sound sleep for at least a year from now unless her parents return from coma. Raising a child is not an easy task. It takes a lot of resilience, patience, and sacrifice. Sia does not have any of this currently but is going to learn very soon.

A newborn child tends to wake up every 2-3 hrs in the night feeling hungry. The child needs to be fed. Some days children can test your patience to the extreme by not sleeping at all and crying endlessly.

Those nights are torture nights. When you have fed the child, carrying the baby in arms, singing lullaby, giving the baby his favourite toys and still baby is in no mood to sleep. This spoils the parents' sleep leading to headache, fatigue, and stomach issues for parents. For at least a year till the child learns to sleep long hours in the night, such situation remains.

In the absence of parents Sia needs to fulfil this duty of waking up in night. For a person who loves her sleep so much, it is going to be a torturous task. As expected, the baby wakes up and starts crying in the middle of the night. Sia who was in deep sleep, especially after looking after the kid the entire day, wakes up in a shock on hearing the baby cry. That sound of baby's cry has become so common that it keeps ringing in her mind even if the baby is not crying. Although Sia has woken up, but her eyes are still 80% closed, she is still completing her half-left dream, partially conscious and partially in dreams, she does not know which world she is living in. It takes few more cries from the baby for Sia to come to more consciousness (still not 100%). She then realises that baby is hungry, goes to the table nearby where everything is placed to quickly make the powder milk and then takes the baby in her laps and feeds him the milk.

While baby was drinking milk, Sia went to partial sleep once again (as she loves her sleep). As soon as the milk is finished, baby starts crying again which wakes Sia up once again. She realises that her job is still not complete and that now she has to make the baby burp and then go to sleep which can involve any kind of activity from standing up and twisting the waist sideways to give the baby a feeling of a swing, sing lullaby, play a calming music on phone, hold the baby with his head resting on your shoulders etc. It is an endless process. You need to produce new innovative ways of making the baby go to sleep.

She tries her best for initial 15 minutes expecting the baby to go to sleep soon. However, destiny had other plans. Tonight is the night of torture, where the baby has decided that he is not going to sleep easily. The baby woke up at 2 AM in the night and it is already 2:45 but no signs of sleeping plus endlessly crying. Sia tried all the tricks she had learnt so far plus a few more with no success. Ultimately, she lost her patience, put the baby on the bed with a little extra force than required purely out of frustration and starts talking rudely to the kid - why are you not sleeping, what wrong have I done, I have given you milk as well, why are you spoiling my sleep? The baby kept crying. She then tried her best to control her emotions and then gave another try for 10-15 mins. Still no success.

It is 4 AM now (2 hours have passed) and the baby is still not sleeping. Sia is sitting on a chair next to the bed with her hands on her forehead in complete despair and irritation. Her head has started aching now. She takes a headache pill as she must take care of the baby somehow. Drops of tears starts flowing out from her eyes. Not to forget she is just a teenager and cannot be expected to behave like adults in such brief period. She is already giving her best, but baby can test anyone's patience. She remembers how she used to shout at her mother when she used to wake her up early morning to get ready for school. She used to scold her for waking her up 15 mins early than the required time and used to go to sleep again in irritation. This was the case just a few days ago and see where she is today. Forget about 15 mins, she is awake since almost 2 hrs in the middle of the night and making a baby sleep. Huge transformation for a teenager.

The tears in her eyes are for more than one reason. One obviously that the baby is not letting her sleep but more importantly the second reason which is she now realises the importance of her mother and parents in general. She misses her mom desperately. She pledges inside her heart that she will never shout at her mother once she comes back. She just wants her to come back and nothing else. She is so emotionally drained out right now that she requires a motherly comfort and love. She is making all the efforts to be brave in such testing situations, but it is still not working. Lot of burden on her suddenly.

After the medicine started showing its effect and her headache subsided, she decided to go for, yet another try. Sia then again took the baby in her arms keeping aside her emotions. She tried to make him go to sleep by giving him comfort and love which she requires right now. It seems like Sia's pain somehow reached God and the baby started getting into sleep in Sia's arms. She can see the baby is yawning, has stopped crying, and gradually going into sleep. Her prayers are honoured, and mission is finally accomplished.

She kept the baby in his bed, put a teddy next to him to make him feel comfortable and then she sat on the chair next to the bed and went to sleep on the chair itself.

Lesson 3 –
Lost Temper

What happens in parenting is, both mother and father have newly become parents, so it is a new experience for them. Raising a child is all together a different ball game. It is not like a new task that a teacher has given which a student can practice and complete, or a boss has given an assignment that you do not have a clue of but still you collaborate with people and figure it out. The only emotion involved in such tasks is stress to understand the problem and as soon as you get it, the task becomes easy.

However, in the case of parenting, it is a human being involved (the kid) with a blood relation and hence a sea of emotions is there, and you cannot afford to go wrong as it will impact a human life. To add fuel to fire, that human being (the kid) will present in front you loads of new challenges on a daily basis of which you do not have a clue and just cannot ask the kid as he or she can only convey their problem in the form of crying. It is like solving a crime case basis the crime scene. You try to decipher what could have happened and develop a story and solution around it.

Similarly, the baby can be hungry, can have stomach-ache or gas, or is hurt, it can be anything. At times it is just that baby wants to cry for no reasons. This is where the test of patience happens for parents. It is not easy at all. One of the world's toughest jobs is to raise a child. One can end up pulling their hairs, shouting out of irritation, or crying along with the baby. All the above happens specially during the first year of parenting as everyone in immature at that time. Child is newly born, and parents are new to parenting.

Something similar happened with Sia as well. In her case one additional element was that she herself was a teenager only, so in general the maturity levels were low, and parenting requires supreme level of maturity and patience, so it was a humongous task for Sia.

During the first year of parenting, there were days when it was too overwhelming for Sia, bathing the child, feeding him, cleaning the shit, making him go sleep and again feed, clean and sleep and repeatedly. It was so tiring for her that she shouted at the baby one evening purely out of frustration. He was vomiting every time Sia tried to feed him some semi solid dal rice. She tried then giving boiled fruit still he vomited. She then tried giving boiled potato he still vomited. Nothing was working. It was evening and the housekeeper has already left so there was no help as well at home. This was all she had, to make him eat. How many more items can someone keep prepared. She thought she had three options ready so it should be more than enough. But this time all options failed. She checked if he was having stomach ache or gas by pressing his belly but that was not the case. Everything seemed fine but he was still not eating. It was several hours since his last meal, so he was hungry for sure. Sia's frustration reached the top when all options failed, and she yelled at his brother for the first time - "what's the matter with you? Even I am a human being. I also need rest, why cannot you have food and go to sleep and let me have my own life as well!" She started crying feeling totally trapped in the situation, no one to help, missing her parents dearly, asked God why he is doing it with her. All her friends are having such a cool life at this age - partying, going on vacation, having food in restaurants etc and here she is parenting a child single handedly without any support at such a tender age of around 14 yrs. No doubt it is a super tough situation for her. God is evaluating her big time. It is not a common scenario.

After some time, while she was crying, she started feeling guilty of yelling at her brother. Nothing strange here. It does happen with matured adults as well. First, they shout and then feel guilty about it. He was crying on his cradle while Sia was sitting next to him in despair.

She then recalled old times when she was too hard on her mother, but her mother never shouted at her such badly. She did raise her voice on Sia but not the way Sia did with her brother. It was too rude and loud. She gathered herself taking motivation from her mother. She picked the baby in her arms and apologized to him. She cuddled him, kissed him, her tears are now all over her brothers face and started singing lullaby and roaming around to make him feel better.

The kid stopped crying after receiving the love and care. Sia saluted her mother in her heart and wondered how she managed to stay calm in such challenging situations. Her admiration for her mother increased manifolds after this incidence. Sia then gave a final try to feed her brother with the evergreen milk. The saviour, the milk. When nothing is working milk comes to rescue and works majority of the time. As soon as she brought the milk bottle close to his brother, he quickly grasped it and started having milk in high speed. He was looking for milk only and did not want to eat anything else. But how do we know. The kid cannot tell, and we can only guess. Trial and error it is. But this trial and error can result in frustration sometimes. This is how parenting is. Nobody can do anything about it. The only thing that a parent can do is to keep calm and have patience.

Eventually issue will get resolved but it might take a toll on your mental health, so it is equally important to relax oneself post going through such traumatic situation in parenting. Sia also did something similar. Post her brother went to sleep, she immediately lied down on bed, put her earphone on and listened to some songs which she loves making her feel a lot better. Additionally, she watched couple of hours of web series on OTT and then went to sleep automatically.

Lesson 4 –
Parenting during periods

On an average a girl's menstrual cycle starts at 12-14 yrs of age. Luckily Sia got introduced to periods while her mother was around and not when she was in coma. It is a horrible experience for a girl when she gets it for the first time. They get deeply scared as its new for them with blood coming out. Thereafter when they get used to it even then those 4-5 days every month are very painful and disgusting. There are hell lot of mood swings ranging from irritation to anger. They must go through extreme pain as well specially at the start. With so many troubles, females around the world continue doing their daily jobs as if nothing has happened. Only they have so much of courage and tolerance.

Sia feels a lot of pain specially on the first day of her periods. It is completely unbearable. She used to skip school on that day every month. She used to just lie down on bed with hot water bag on her stomach with mom giving her comfort. She ends up crying every time as well.

With such a history, Sia was scared to the core as her time for the period was arriving and this time, she was a parent herself. Her mother being in coma, there was no one to give her comfort in these tough days. On the contrary, she had to give comfort to the kid digesting all the pain that she would be going through. She was not sure how will she do it. There would be housekeeper to help however the kid needs Sia most of the time. Hence many a times the housekeeper feels helpless with the kid not going to her and only needing Sia. She is still very new to parenting and has not developed that kind of patience which is required in parenting.

For the past couple of days Sia was feeling irritated and there was slight pain as well. She realised that soon she will get her periods. One day the pain increased exponentially. It was unbearable and she took to bed. She was just not able to move and wanted to lie down all the time. Raghav started crying and wanted Sia only. Nothing can pacify him except Sia while she lied on the bed almost lifeless. She was in deep pain. She was getting super irritated on the sound of Raghav's cry. It was hitting her brain hard, the sound of cry. She wanted to be at peace but with a kid in house that is the last thing you can expect. Sia then asked the housekeeper to keep Raghav next to her on the bed and she tried to calm her down halfheartedly by rubbing her hands on his head. The cry did go down. She asked the housekeeper to prepare milk and give her. She then put the milk bottle in his mouth while lying next to her on bed. He then started drinking milk peacefully with some relief for Sia as well. After finishing the milk, she asked the housekeeper to put his cradle next to her bed and put Raghav in it. She then swung the cradle with one hand while lying on bed. All the time, Raghav was looking at Sia with eager eyes asking to take him in arms. He felt a motherly affection in Sia. Raghav did cry initially but Sia did not have the strength to stand and take him in her arms and make him go to sleep. So, she tried this short cut method. After 5-10 mins of resistance, Raghav went to sleep. Sia then took a sign of relief and asked the housekeeper to look after the baby while she also takes a small nap.

It was just the start of the day, and many other activities were left where Sia had to deal with the pain and the kid both simultaneously. Sia asked the housekeeper to bathe the kid and take him for a ride in the stroller. This way some more time will pass. Housekeeper then gave some food for Sia to have as she had not had anything since morning and its already lunch time. She ate half of it somehow and left the remaining. The entire stress of managing the kid and the pain was playing on her mind. Half of the day is gone with the help of the housekeeper however she was not able to do the night duty. So, she asked the housekeeper for a favour to stay back for one night. The housekeeper felt it was a genuine ask from Sia looking at her condition and immediately agreed. Sia then felt much better mentally.

As pain subsided for some time in the evening she looked after the kid playing with him while he was lying on the bed. The blood flow had started, and she wore the pad. She was feeling disgusted from below but tried her best to control her emotions. She thought how her mom used to work tirelessly during her periods. Many a times Sia will not even know that her periods are going on. She managed it so effortlessly. Sia thought why cannot she do it as well. She is making a big issue out of it. On getting this thought she asked herself to roll her sleeves and come out of self-pity. She remembered her mother, gathered the courage, and started looking after the baby like a regular day. She took him in her arms, swung him sideways by twisting her waist. It was painful but still she did it. She walked around the house carrying him to make him feel good. She made milk for him and fed him. She also took care of her brother by waking up in the night even if the housekeeper was there. The housekeeper asked her to rest but she was adamant. She did not want to be in that state of pity. She did not like it.

She was trying to be like her mom. The respect for her mother's efforts multiplied several times in her heart. She wondered how ignorant she was earlier of her mother's efforts. She should have given love and care to her when she went through her periods. But she never did. She was only bothered about her pain. She felt really annoyed at her own self. How terrible she was in understanding emotions of people around her. She then promised herself that she will always try to control her emotions and give importance to other feelings specially her family.

Lesson 5 –
Baby gets fever

As it happens with every child, when he faces the external environment after birth, he can fall sick as he is overly sensitive and due to various toxic element present in outside environment. He is a newly born and does not have its own immunity yet. It is getting developed each day. Outside cold, pollution, toxins etc can quickly affect the child's health. No matter how much you keep the baby protected somehow, he finds the way to fall sick. It is the case with everyone.

Similar stuff happened with Sia and her brother as well. Due to the changing weather outside, the kid developed cough and cold along with fever. He finds it difficult to breathe due to congestion and has become very cranky. Being just 4-5 months old, the kid really does not know how to express his health problems apart from crying. He is crying continuously. Sia takes him to nearby paediatrician for consultation. She buys the prescribed medicine. It is Sia's first time looking after someone in the family when he or she is ill. Till now she has not faced any such responsibility. Every time she was the one who used to fall sick, and parents used to take care. In case any of the parents used to fall sick then the other parent used to take care with no responsibility on Sia. So, like everything else this was also a completely new experience. Managing an illness of a family member and that too of a 4–5-month-old kid is one of the toughest things to do as the ill person cannot even tell you his problem and you just must feel and sense it and take appropriate decisions.

Sia showed a lot of courage and dealt with the situation with utmost bravery. She took the right steps at the right time making sure the illness does not aggravate further. Doctor has done all the check-ups and has prescribed the medicine, which has given some relief to the kid. Earlier the kid was not accepting milk as he was not able to drink it due to nose blockage. Post medication, some of the congestion came out and baby felt some relief and accepted some milk.

Managing the kid for few months now, Sia has grown a lot mentally. She is gradually becoming a seasoned parent, experiencing every situation one after the other which a new parent goes through.

But how come she pulled it off so nicely. Why did not she get irritated or frustrated at all. Well, it is because right at the start she remembered how her mother took care of her when she was ill. Every single time when she was ill her mother used to take care of her like a small baby giving all the love in this world. She would make all the food Sia loves, will take care of her medicines, make her fall asleep on her laps and all that a mother does. She remembers how comforting it was and how she used to go into another world in her mother's lap. It was the best feeling in the world. All this she recalled right at the start and wanted to give the same to her brother. All the love she gave to the kid, he responded back very nicely and felt the same comfort which helped him to recover fast. Love had a bigger impact than any medicines. This again shows how much emotional turmoil a parent goes through while parenting. It is a sea of emotions. Love anger irritation care possessiveness all at once.

Lesson 6 –
Ear piercing

The old housekeeper one day during a casual conversation with Sia told her that a child piercing is done in their village at a very nascent stage ranging from just a couple of months of age to 6 months of age. This is because the child's skin is delicate and soft at that time and hence piercing can be done with least amount of pain. Sia also remembered her mother saying in the past that in their family it is a tradition to get the ears pierced at an early age irrespective of the gender of the child. It is an age-old ritual in their family. Both the housekeeper and the mother's version reconciled in Sia's mind which made her take the decision of getting Raghav's ear pierced.

As usual, every event causes Sia to go through a mix of emotions in her heart. She was excited to get her brothers ears pierced and already started thinking about the design of the stud. But at the same time, she was really worried about the amount of pain that her brother will have to go through. Will there be too much blood? will he cry a lot? She thought about all such points in her head at least one thousand times to evaluate what should she do. Is it important to get ear piercing done? Afterall he is a boy so is it really required in this case? She tried to produce reasons not to go ahead to avoid any pain to her brother. But at the same time, she wanted to fulfil the family tradition as well. After a lot of thought, she finally gave tradition more weightage. In the absence of parents, she does not want to break any traditions.

She now realises why was her mother so stressed out all the time and always lost in thoughts. She has the answer to yet another question she had regarding her mom's behaviour which she could not ask directly. All of it seems so right now, now she finds herself in that same spot. It is she who is stressed and lost all the time. Initially she thought that it is just carelessness of her mother but now she realises that it was nothing but the welfare of her child and family in general that occupied her mind all the time. She apologized to her mom in her heart for thinking about her behaviour in the wrong direction.

So finally, after deciding in favour of piercing, she went to the nearby jewellery store, the owner of which already knows her parents very well. Her mom used to buy jewellery from this shop only. Sia asked to show all the options available for her brother and then chose a gold wire with a stud. The owner himself was going to do the piercing. He asked Sia to hold the baby tight specially his head and hands so that he does not make any movement while the piercing is being done. The shop owner marked a small spot with a pen on the ear where he is going to pierce. So finally, the moment has arrived. He places the gold wire near the baby's ear. As soon as he did that, the expression on Sia's face were unmatched. It was a mix of fright and tension as she knew what will happen once that wire goes in.

He quickly within fraction of a second presses it and the wire pierces the ear and comes out from the other end. The baby could not even realise what has happened but the very next second he started crying out of pain. He quickly pierced the second ear as well while the baby was crying out loudly with everyone around watching the show. He then twisted the wire from behind the ear and cut the sharp end to make it rounded. Here you go, piercing is done and a big task completed. Sia quickly pays the bill and thanks the owner and leaves the shop as the baby was crying endlessly. Sia comforted the baby at home and made him go to sleep. From inside Sia was also crying watching Raghav in so much pain. This episode made her realise what goes through a mom when her child is in pain and when she must take some critical decisions which might give temporary pain to the child but is good eventually.

Sia was facing such dilemma and irony for the first time in life. She knows it is going to be painful, yet she had to take that step. She was never such confused earlier. She realized how difficult it is for parents to take certain decisions and so easy it is to criticize the outcome of those decisions. She herself has criticized her parents' multiple times for various things. She wondered if Raghav were able to talk and would have shouted at her for getting his ears pierced how would have, she reacted. There were chances she would have shouted back at him making the situation ugly. She quietly admired her mother in her heart for managing all such similar situations so gracefully without shouting. She then realized that she has a long way to become a matured adult.

Lesson 7 –
First steps

Sia has been studying about parenting from internet every day. This has helped her to navigate through these tough times of parenting. Apart from internet she only had the old housekeeper to guide. Housekeeper is also not aware about the changed ways of parenting with new age and some of the latest ways of parenting. The housekeeper still follows certain traditional methods which nowadays the doctor advice not to do. Things like applying kajal in eyes are not advised by doctors however the housekeeper insisted on doing it. This is where internet and consulting the paediatrician comes in handy.

Now the baby being into his 10th month, Sia wanted to make efforts towards making him walk a few steps at least. She has read that by this time baby should be walking a few steps or at least make some efforts toward it. Some suggested to use walker however with new ways of parenting a lot of new age parents are avoiding walkers and trying to make the baby walk on their own with some support. Sia also preferred avoiding the walker at least initially and in case she feels the need later then she will go for it. She started making the baby stand on the floor holding her hands and then making a small move away from the child forcing him to follow her by taking a step. The baby responded well by taking that first step which filled Sia with joy and confidence that she can pull it off. However, it required doing this regularly several times a day to make the baby habitual. This could be tiring and required lot of patience. But Sia was adamant. She wanted to make sure that her brother starts walking at the right time not too early or late. She then regularly held her brothers hand making him stand and then moving away from him forcing to make a move. After several successful attempts she decided to gradually take away her hands making him stand on his own. As soon as she did this, he remained standing however with shaky legs and dropped on the floor after few seconds. She continued this practice for several days and his performance improved. He can now stand longer on his own without any support and makes genuine attempt to take a step forward. But as soon as he takes a step he falls. After few more days of practice he can now take a couple of steps without any support making Sia feel proud that her efforts are paying off.

One day she became quite aggressive in her efforts and pushed the kid to take more than couple of steps. When he completed two steps Sia continued pushing him to move further and did not give any support. This led to the baby falling on the floor hitting his face on the ground and getting hurt on the nose and mouth. There was slight blood also coming out of his mouth. Sia panicked and immediately gave him first aid and started pacifying the crying baby. She scolded herself internally as to why did she push him so hard. It was because of her that he got injured. The baby was also angry with her and was not coming in her arms. After lot of efforts and persuasion he came in her arms and then she sang him a lullaby.

This reminded her of an incidence where she was on a family outing with parents on a hilly station. There was some trekking involved as well but not much. It was a flattish trek which was walkable with shops on both sides. They all were doing the trek together happily with excitement of reaching their luxurious resort. A lot of fun was waiting for them. Sia was moving ahead while looking at the shops on the side of the trek. She did not realise that there was a rock in front of her. Her foot hit the rock, and she tumbled. Her mother was right next to her and by the time she reacted and reached out to hold Sia, she has already fallen and injured herself slightly.

As usual she was instant in shouting at her mother in irritation while her mother tried to give her first aid and being apologetic at the same time. She scolded her mother for not saving her and did not talk to her that entire day. She now regrets this inappropriate behaviour of hers towards her mother when she herself is managing a kid. She now realises how is it to be a mom. She felt bad when her brother neglected her and did not want to come in her laps as he was angry with her.

Trivia – As you sow so shall you reap!!

Sia got a glimpse of how it is to be on the other side of the table. She now knows how it feels when a child is angry with their parent. It is an ugly feeling. A parent can never feel bad about their child. Even if they are angry, a parent will always think good about their child. Whereas a child will revolt with their parents when he is angry and will not listen to them making them feel worse. Such is a relation between parent and their children in general.

After many such tough situations in her parenting journey, Sia promised never to be angry with her parents. Never ever! If she cannot take care of them then at least she should not give more pain to them by shouting at them or by any of her actions.

Lesson 8 –
1st birthday

Hooray!! The baby is going to be 1 year old very soon. Yes, his first birthday is near. It has been almost 9 months since Sia is parenting. What a ride it has been. It is a 360° transformation for Sia. In this short span of time, one can see remarkable difference in Sia. She is already behaving like an adult parent. She follows a proper routine now. Waking up at 7AM in the morning along with the baby. Brushes hers and her brother's teeth (whatever few are there). She can now manage him with one hand and do the rest of the work simultaneously with the other hand. She has become a pro!! That is life. No better teacher than life itself. One can give it a name of Museebat University. When you are in trouble you automatically learn a lot as if you are studying in a proper university.

She feeds the baby with some semi solid food like mashed fruits, potato, or veggies, sometimes dal rice. She does her breakfast with one hand holding the 1yr old in the other. Oh man! It is an impressive growth. Even the old housekeeper is shocked at times to see such tremendous changes in her. She then bathes the baby, make him wear smart clothes and then takes him for a walk in the park outside. Makes him play with the swings and rides. He has started walking a few steps as well which is a happy progress. The boy is healthy and is doing excellent health wise all thanks to our little parent Sia who is no littler. Comes back home and feeds the baby again and makes him go to sleep in the afternoon. She also takes rest at that time. Once he wakes up in the afternoon, she again feeds him with other varieties of food which he likes, plays building block game with him, have a fun run around the house with the baby crawling all around, then again go out to park for some more activities and come back home, have dinner and some milk and put the baby to sleep.

Entire life dedicated to this pure bundle of joy with absolutely no regret. She loves it this way. She has started loving this life now after crossing the torturous initial phase. She has accepted the situation and has made peace with it. She no longer questions it or fights with destiny. She has accepted it that it must be god's way of teaching her and making her stronger. She now accepts challenges with a smile and open arms. It has been 9 months since her parents are in coma. She goes to visit them every day. It is a daily ritual now. She does not feel comfortable in taking the baby with her so goes alone only. Earlier she used to fight with God to cure them quickly otherwise she would get angry etc but now she just prays for their good and stable health and accepts that whenever God wants, they will come back to life.

Well, kids first birthday is near and Sia wish to celebrate it in a grand fashion. In a way it is also a celebration of Sia's parenting efforts and efficient management of the crisis. It has been quite a journey. She arranges for birthday decoration at home, ordered a lovely cake and food from a local caterer and invited few of her school friends and neighbours. Being the first birthday of her brother, she wants to make it memorable. She has even written a song or a poem also which she will sing on his brothers' birthday. She is very emotional about this event. She just wants her brother to enjoy and smile.

The birthday finally arrives. The decoration team arrived in the morning to start decorating the living area. Sia checked with the caterer, and he confirmed that food is getting ready and will be on time. Around that time the cake also got delivered. Sia is feeling comfortable now with most of the arrangement taking shape as per her expectation. It around 5pm and it is party time. Guests have started arriving and the party is slowly picking pace. Snacks are being served; kids are playing fun games while everyone is waiting for cake cutting. It is a fun atmosphere with kids running around and playing with toys, parents are chatting with each other while having snacks.

Finally, the chief guest of the party Sia's little brother Raghav arrives all dressed up in jeans and shirt along with sunglasses looking dashing and cute. Everyone showers their love to him by giving hugs and kisses. Sia has deliberately put a "kala tika" on his forehead to avoid bad omen.

Sia now makes him cut the cake while everyone sings happy birthday. It is such a cute and lovely moment. Sia then thought that it is the perfect time to sing the small poem she wrote in front of everyone:

"You changed my life upside down.

You brought my attitude to the ground.

You filled my life with loads of love.

My heart is filled with full of care.

May God keep our bond forever strong.

May he also keep you healthy and strong?

You are my heart; you are my soul.

Happy first birthday my little bro"

Everyone clapped after listening to this sweet little poem. All praised Sia for writing such a cute poem.

Though there were lot of gifts which guests have brought for Raghav, but little did anyone know that Mr Raghav himself have planned a return gift for her sister Sia. Yes, this cute little 1 yr old boy did something which absolutely surprised everyone and specially her sister Sia. This one small act of her brother surpassed everything that Sia did for his birthday. Raghav gave his sister the most wonderful gift that any parent can get. While everyone was having cake and celebrating, Raghav utters a proper word for the first time in his life on his birthday and that was "Ma". Yes, he called her sister Sia "Ma". Oh my god! Sia was all in tears. These are tears of happiness and joy. Can any gift be better than this one. She immediately hugged her brother and gave numerous kisses. Everyone jumped and danced with joy. Sia sang a song for Raghav with an even bigger smile on her face. It was totally a memorable day. No one was happier than Sia. She now realised how can a single word bring such a joy in life. This is what happens to parents. They do not want anything big. These small moments are all they want. Some small moments of love and affection that they get from their children is more than enough to make their day. This is exactly what Sia felt today. Additionally, she promised that the day her parents will come to life again, she will make sure she gives such moments of love and care to them daily to make them feel special. Another great lesson from the University of parenting.

Lesson 9 –
Baby boy hides behind dining table

Just a regular day was going on, housekeeper was in kitchen preparing food for both the children, Sia in the meantime told her to look after Raghav while she quickly goes to take a shower. Raghav was playing with his toys in living area of the house. There is a wall mounted 55-inch TV on one wall with L shaped lounger on the opposite wall. This is one section of the large living area. In the other section there is dining table with two sides of the dining table having a wall behind it and the other two side are facing the TV and lounger. So, there is that one corner behind the dining table where the two walls meet, that is a blind spot of the house. It any toy or other item goes inside that area then the entire dining table needs to be shifted to take out that item.

So, while the housekeeper went to kitchen to look after the food which was cooking and Sia taking shower, Raghav crawled toward that area of dining table and sat exactly in that corner below the dining table hiding behind the chairs. He is not visible even if one glares the dining table by bending down as he has covered himself with a towel which was lying around. When housekeeper comes back, she panics on not seeing Raghav anywhere. She screamed, Sia was also ready by then she immediately rushed downstairs to check with housekeeper what happened. They both started looking at all the possible places where Raghav can be but with no success. They both panicked and almost started crying as well. They were both cursing themselves why did they leave the baby alone, they should not have done that, oh god please help. The main door was open by chance which made Sia panic even more as she thought that Raghav has crawled out of the house. She rushed outside the house and checked the lobby area. No signs of Raghav. She then told herself that she is being too pessimistic here and that there are high chances that he is inside the house only hiding somewhere.

She then prayed to God to help her in finding her brother. It was then Raghav coughed and Sia heard it. She tried to figure out from where the voice came. She quickly realised that it might have come from somewhere near the dining table and that was one area which they did not check properly.

Without thinking twice Sia immediately dragged the dining slowly outwards making some space to enter that blind spot and there he was hiding and covering himself with towel making exceedingly difficult to find. They felt a sign of relief. Sia picked Raghav in her arms and hugged and kissed him. Housekeeper also hugged Raghav. They politely scolded Raghav in a lovable fashion that he should not do it again and should always be with them. They also scolded themselves and promised that they are not going to leave him alone from now on for not even a second.

Sia could not have afforded to lose yet another family member. Raghav is her only hope in case her parents do not return. That is why She is utmost possessive about him. She can do anything for her brother. It is more of a mother son relationship than of siblings. The parental feeling further solidified in Sia's heart and mind post this incidence. Day by day every such event is making her more of a mother than a sister. Day by day, Sia's love and care for her brother is only increasing with no looking back. Her parents would have been enormously proud of her and this relationship. They would have cried out of joy.

Lesson 10 –
Fasting for baby

As Sia was playing with her brother in a park one day, she overheard a group of women discussing about the fast tomorrow which is kept for the welfare of their kid. It is called Sakat Chauth. She immediately recalls that her mother used to keep a fast every year and she used to say that it is for your good. She also recalled that it was around this time of the year only. She was confirmed now. Thanks to the ladies, she came to know that tomorrow is that fast. Without any second thought she decided that she will be keeping that fast for her brother but as his mother. She has already started feeling happy and excited about it. But it is not going to be easy. She has never kept a fast till now in her life. Not even once. As we remember our old Sia, she was modern and followed western culture and was not so fond of such religious traditions. My God! look at her now, she decides to keep this fast in a second without a second thought. This is what parenting does to you. It changes you completely. You become a better version of yourself. Sia's parents would have been super proud to see such admirable changes in her.

She confirms about the fast from the old housekeeper and she also confirms that it is tomorrow. She discusses with the housekeeper what all needs to be done ranging from what to wear, how to do pooja, what can she eat and when can she eat etc. Shockingly, now that she is decided she comes to know that is it not a regular fast, but it is a "Nirjala vrat" meaning no water. OMG! What to do now for a person who has never observed a fast in her life and is going to do a fast that too without water. It is going to be one of her biggest tests. The odds are all against her - never kept a fast, cannot drink water, she is a foodie by nature, she must look after the kid in that condition. On the face of it seems like a nightmare. But she is still ready to take a chance. She does all the preparation for tomorrow's fast.

The next day is finally here. Sia wakes up remembering that today she must make everyone proud and not to fail in fasting. She decided to keep herself busy to avoid thinking about food. She does all the daily activity along with the pooja for the day. She also decides that she will speak less so that she does not feel thirsty and conserves energy.

It was all fine till lunch time around 12-1 pm. It was then when she started feeling hungry. The boy was also asleep so she could not engage in playing with him. So, she took her mobile and played a web series to divert her mind. It was then she realises that she left this series when her parents met with an accident, and it is now that she is resuming to watch it again after so many months. She has not touched this web series ever since that incident. She devoted her entire time to her brother. A commendable job. She started watching from where she left. This helped in passing one more hour. Half of the day is gone now, and few hours are left post which she can offering prayers to the moon, complete the rituals, and can have her meal.

After controlling for so many hours since morning, she was not able to control her hunger and her thirst at all. She produced an idea and asked Maid to look after the kid while she takes a nap. This will help in passing yet another hour or so. As she was perpetually tired after so many days of parenting she can get sleep in any condition even empty stomach. Housekeeper took over the kid and she went to sleep in her room. The moment she woke up and saw her watch, 2 hours were gone. Hurray! She thought of passing one hour but ended up spending 2 hours in sleep. Evening is approaching fast and now she can start preparation for the pooja and other rituals. Along with that she played with her brother and fed him snacks which kept her busy. And here you go, the time for moon rise has come. Oh, my goodness, she has almost done it. She tightly hugged her brother in celebration of this effort of hers which she specially did for her brother but as a mother. It was special for Sia. She then did the prayers and offering to the moon and then had her meal. Like Karwa Chauth, Sia made Raghav feed him first bite and some water to break her fast. It felt so special to her. Raghav also enjoyed it. She did it! First fast of her life and that too without water. What a commendable job!

At around midnight when Raghav was fast asleep, she was thinking about the day that just passed and about her parents. Her admiration for her mother increased manifolds yet again post this fast. She recalled that her mother used to work tirelessly even during this fast. How was she able to do it. Is she human or an avatar of God. Sia gave her mother the stature of a God in her heart after this day and really started missing her. She cried as well in her mother's memory. Life has taken such an unusual turn for her. She is just a teenager and is going through so much. Her efforts are truly commendable. Her heart which was filled with self-love, now believes in only giving love. She cried all night at the balcony. She never thought life will take such a turn. She missed her parents badly. She desperately wanted someone to hug her and make her go to sleep in their laps. Only parents can give such comfort, where you forget all the worries of the world. She begged God to return her parents to her promising that she will be a good girl all her life in return for this favour.

She has understood the value of parents completely in the past 1 year.

Lesson 11 –
First hug

Baby 1yr 3 months old and till now has achieved several necessary milestones like saying words "maa", "pa", walking a few steps, eating semi solid food, teeth growth is good etc. Day by day things are getting better for Sia as she herself is much more experienced now plus baby is also progressing well and cooperating better.

What is overwhelming for Sia is too much of giving and not receiving anything. Meaning all the time she must attend another person (kid in this case), provide all types of care and comfort to him without receiving anything in return. There is no one to take care of her, old housekeeper does the basic things but cannot provide emotional support for obvious reasons. She was in desperate need for some love and care herself. After all she is also human. It has been 1 yr now since she has been parenting. It is a big journey that is she has covered. She misses her parents every single moment of her life. She now realises their importance even more. She knows that they were the only ones who could have given her the emotional support she needs the most right now. How can she expect something from a year-old child. Her only solace is few moments of smile and laughter with the kid. This is all she gets to rejuvenate herself. Her life has become extremely monotonous as compared to her previous life where it was difficult to find her at home. All the time she was outside either in school or at friend's place or partying around. She was such a social person and look at her now, she has become the most private person in her age group with absolutely no social life. It has been ages she has talked to her friends as well. Burden of responsibility has taken over her so much that she feels guilty talking on phone with friends thinking she is not looking after the child. She either does not pick up their calls or if she answers then disconnects the phone quickly making excuses relating to the kid. Her friends also give her benefit of doubt and do not say much. One time a close friend of hers came to visit her at home. That friend was there at Sia's home for quite some time and saw that all the time she is busy with the kid and not able to have normal conversation with her. From then on, her friend realised that Sia has other important stuff to do and rightly so, hence it is their moral duty to not come in its way and let her do it. Whole life is there, they can cover up for this lost time later but now her priority should be the kid. So, they stopped coming to her home. But all this while their friendship was intact even if there was no communication whatsoever.

This is a common phenomenon. New parents tend to become asocial for quite some time specially during the first year of birth and specially if no elderly support is there. Then as time passes by, gradually they start going out with friends and family. Partly due to this reason that some mothers go through depression also as their life changes 360°. At such a point in life all that a parent wants is some care and emotional support from their loved ones.

However, in Sia's case no one was there. No family, only she and her brother were left. Her brother is too small to expect anything from him. But hey that is when the magic happens. May be the kid felt it or God knows how, while Sia was sitting on a mat on the floor and Raghav was few steps away from her, he stood up taking support from sofa and took those few steps towards Sia and hugged her by falling on her with a big smile saying "Maa". OMG!! How did he know that this is what Sia was looking for. Some love warmth and affection. Children are God's avatar. They have highly active senses and can feel the environment of the house. Sia's emotions must have been felt by him, and he did what he could in such a small age. A hug. Yes, after all this is what anyone needs when depressed. This was his first hug to Sia which he initiated himself. Otherwise generally Sia makes the first move. But this time it was her brother. All the depression vanished at least for that moment and gave Sia some more energy to move on in life.

This made her realize that parenting is not particularly bad. It gives you moments of immense joy and love as well. It gives you feelings that cannot be expressed in words. It is simply magical at times.

Lesson 12 –
Introduction to real parents

Sia thought that it would be very unfair on her part if she projects herself as the mother and does not introduce Raghav to his real parents. She is still not comfortable to take him to the hospital due to several reasons, but she can at least show their photo to him at home and ask him to address them as Ma and Pa.

By this time Raghav has already started calling Sia Ma, so it is going to be even more typical to make him unlearn that. So Sia decided why cannot he just call both as Ma. So even if he calls Sia Ma, she can show the pic of his real mother and ask him to call her Ma as well. As soon as this thought came to her mind, she brought a photo of all of them which was hanging on the wall and started introducing Raghav to each member.

When she pointed her finger to herself in the photo, Raghav immediately sprung with Joy and said Ma. It was such an adorable and memorable moment for Sia. She absolutely loved it. How fast was Raghav in recognising Sia in the photo and the enthusiasm with which he said Ma was so lovely. Sia found it so cute that she gave him lots of hugs and kisses. She then pointed towards her father and asked Raghav to say Pa. After making several efforts, he said Pa. By now he was comfortable saying Ma, Pa, Baba etc so it was easy for him. Sia then revised his learning by pointing the finger to their father and asking Raghav who is he. After a pause of few seconds, he said Pa. This reassured Sia that he has learnt it well. So, Pa is done.

Now comes the tricky one. How to do this. He already highlighted Sia as Ma all by himself so how to attach that same word with another person who is his Ma. Nevertheless, Sia gave a try by pointing her finger towards their mother and asking him to say Ma. As soon as he heard Ma, he immediately turned his head towards Sia further clarifying that for him it is Sia who is Ma. She then gave another try by saying "yeh bhi Ma hai". So, she tried to convey that she is also Ma and Sia is also Ma. It took several attempts to make him learn that, but finally he did it. When pointed to either Sia or their mother for he started saying Ma so that is a win for Sia. She now feels much more relaxed and there is no guilt in her mind that she has taken the position of her mother although she deserves that respect after all the efforts, she has put in.

It was a very noble thought of Sia. She has learnt to give value that the other person deserves. She hates to take anybody else's credit. In contrast, the previous version of Sia was all about being in limelight even if it requires to outshine her close friends. This nature of hers have totally reversed now and she believes in putting others in limelight, giving credit and appreciation. This is true sign of a leader which she has learnt. Such humbleness will take her a long way.

Lesson 13 – Mandir

Sia wanted to add a spiritual angle to her parenting by familiarising Raghav with Hindu Gods. At least if he can identify them when the name of a God is taken or can say a portion of the name of God if not in full in his own toddler language that also will be a win for Sia. She thought about this as she has observed that her father was deeply religious and spiritual and followed Sanatani traditions judiciously. So, she wanted that legacy to continue and earlier the start the better it is.

So, she decided to take him to the nearby Iskcon temple. It was a 10 min autorickshaw ride from home. They got ready and hired an autorickshaw and sat in it. It was yet another game for Raghav. This was his first autorickshaw ride and he just could not hold back his excitement. He started fidgeting around and touching all the instruments, rod, cushion etc to touch and feel them. One more aspect of parenting that Sia got introduced recently was answering questions. As the child grows, he tends to ask numerous questions sometimes same question repeatedly to fulfil his curiosity. This can lead to frustration in parents. Since autorickshaw ride was full of new things and he has recently started saying couple of words like "yeh kya" meaning what is this. He pointed out to the red coloured reading on the meter and said in his toddler tone "yeh kya". Sia told him that it is a meter, red coloured are the numbers etc. almost half the journey was spent in explaining the entire meter to him repeatedly. He went on asking the same question about the meter. Every time Sia tried to answer in a separate way to make him understand in simple language, but he kept on asking same question again as if he was doing it deliberately to annoy Sia. Even the autorickshaw driver had a smile on his face listening

Sia explain the meter to Raghav. Not sure how much he understands and thank God for Sia his attention finally got diverted to traffic outside and the meter thing ended. He then continued pointing to various cars and bikes and asking "yeh kya" and the perpetual question answer session continued.

Finally, the destination arrived. They entered the temple, took off their shoes and went inside. There Sia introduced Raghav to Radha and Krishna ji. He even tried to say Radha in his toddler tone as "Lada". That was a small achievement for Sia. She then showed him around, drawing his attention to various images carved on the walls. All those images attracted him a lot and he kept gazing at them endlessly. They then sat inside and enjoyed the kirtan that was going on. Raghav also clapped his hands and enjoyed the kirtan. They then went down to have some holy prasad. As it was spicy, she could not give to Raghav. They clicked some pictures near a big image of Krishna Bhagwan.

Overall, it was a wonderful experience. Sia felt proud of herself that she was able to introduce Hindu Gods to Raghav and that all went so well. She thought in her mind that her parents would have felt proud of her for doing this. She could imagine her parents standing in front of her and giving their blessings. She started feeling emotional as well. She genuinely thought that this was one of her best initiatives till now. There are many more such initiatives that she will have to take in future to groom the child.

Trivia - Parenting involves lot of trial and error to finally achieve the goal.

Lesson 14 –
Baby makes Sia recall her father

A regular day was going on, where Sia was playing with her brother who is almost 2 yr old now. He was sitting beside his sister while playing with blocks. Sia could see Raghav's right side of the face as he was sitting on her left. Sia was also simultaneously playing with blocks making modern designs to impress her brother and make him happy. She then turned her head and looked at her brother just casually. Raghav had the same side face and smile as his father. It immediately reminded Sia of him. As if she was siting besides her father. Her eyes stuck for a moment, and she kept on staring at her brother feeling nostalgic.

Kids do tend to look like their parents a lot which is naturally so. It happens that sometimes they look extremely like their parents. Like a carbon copy. It can be side profile or front profile, or hairstyle, or smile or eyes or overall look. It does happen. Parents also feel that their kid is looking like them and they start feeling proud and all the happier about it. It gives them a sense of goodness somehow.

In another incidence, Raghav was standing near the door waiting for Sia to come and help him wear shoes as they were going out to park. When Sia arrived, she bent down and took one shoe in her hand and asked Raghav to raise his one leg so that she can put in the shoe. So, Raghav feeling that he will fell if he raises his one leg, he automatically put his one hand on Sia's shoulder and then raised his leg. This caught Sia's imagination. Once Sia's father was having a backache and Sia helped him wear his shoes. His father also put his hand on Sia's shoulder in the exact same fashion. It might be that everyone will do the same but since she has experienced it before with her father, when Raghav did it, it had an emotional impact on her.

According to Sia, the touch was the same, even the speed at which the hand approach towards her, the facial expression at that time everything was the same. This again reminded Sia for her father.

There are many more such instances.

Her father liked eating raw ice cubes directly from the freezer. Once Raghav came across an ice cube in some drink and he had it. Instantly he became a fan of ice cubes and wanted to have it daily just like his father.

Whenever Sia felt that her brother looked or did things like his father, she started feeling very full from inside. She was reminded of her father, and she started feeling emotional. A drop of tears started developing around her eyes. It was an overwhelming feeling. She wished his dad were here. She would have hugged him and would have felt so relaxed. She was always every fond her father and felt comfortable while he was around. She is missing him dearly. Once again, we can see how a small glimpse of a child can start a tsunami of emotions in a parent (in this case it was Sia). Such is parenting, each day each event can make you go through so much emotional turmoil which can become beyond control at times. Love care anger irritation all at once. Parenting just takes you to another level as a person. It grooms you to become an adult in the shortest span of time which no university can do.

Lesson 15 –
Don't watch too much TV

Sia has always been fond of watching TV. Her watch list ranged from cartoons, movies to web series on OTT. It is a wide range. Therefore, she was glued to TV most of the times after coming back from school. She did not used to have her meals properly; she never did her homework, and she did not even study much. She is either glued to TV or chatting with friends on mobile or out of home partying or hanging around with them.

This annoyed her parents specially her mom a lot. She always used to scold her for doing this and wanted her to focus on her studies. She always complained that it will have an impact on her eye health as well. Which happened and she was prescribed eyeglasses at an early age.

Now karma has hit Sia. Raghav has developed a strong liking towards cartoons and TV in general. Sia initially started making him watch kids rhymes, ABCD/1234, animals etc to introduce things to him, which has now developed into a strong habit. Based on the research that Sia did on parenting, few minutes of TV is helpful to increase the knowledge of the kid. They catch things visually faster than just telling verbally. Sia used to do the same using knowledge books for toddlers. However, he got bored very easily with the books and whenever Sia used to make him go through the books he used to resist. In TV he was able to see more range of stuff which he loved. If not given his regular dose of TV, then he becomes cranky and cries a lot. Like many other children, he needs to watch TV while eating otherwise he will not. Even after watching TV for an hour, if Sia closes the TV Raghav starts crying loudly.

Sia felt clueless on how to stop this screen addiction of Raghav. She cursed herself for introducing TV to him. She did not expect this to happen. One method which she tried to curb his screen time is by spending more time in the park. She almost forced him to play with as many rides as possible and spent a lot of time in park. This way he got tired as well as hungry. Both of the above are good for him. Feeling hungry is good as he will do less tantrums while eating and getting tired makes him go to sleep easily. It did help in reducing the screen time however it is not completely gone. He still needs TV while eating at least. Also, when Sia is frustrated of looking after the kid for long time she switches the TV on to get a breather.

She now understands what her mother went through. It was her concern for Sia that made her do it. All the while Sia thought that her mother does not want her to relax and chill and always wants her to study. But that was not the case. Her mother would have easily given her time to chill if she had completed her homework and studies. But since she was always lacking in her studies, her mother kept on pushing her to study. As far as Sia is concerned, she always considered that her mother is the villain and does not love her anymore.

Trivia - Kids incorrectly equate tough behaviour of parents to lack of love. That is never the case. Love is always there; they just want you to succeed in life.

Similarly, Sia was fine with Raghav watching the TV for some time if Raghav did not show tantrums while eating or lack of interest in playing with toys. She did not want her physical efforts to go down because of TV. As of now Sia is continuing her effort to reduce screen time with small success each day. It is an ongoing process. One habit goes another comes. Sia is unaware of it. She will have to deal with many other habits in future. She needs to be tactful in dealing with them.

Lesson 16 –
Another boy hurts Raghav

As part of the daily schedule, Sia takes Raghav to park for an outing as well as some play in the kids play area. The play area is very well built with all types of rides to keep the kids engaged and excited. From slides, to see saw, ladders, merry go round, swings, it has it all. Multiple types of each ride are available. So, if one swing is occupied there are five others available. It is a big park able to accommodate many kids at once.

Naturally, lot of families bring their kids to this park, so it is always crowded. Only during the afternoon lunch hours is the park empty else all the time there are kids playing around. At times there is a waiting line for few popular rides. In addition to the kids play area, there is a large walking area surrounded by lush greenery, with bushes cut into the shape of animals like elephant, horse, butterfly to attract the attention of kids. There are artificial cows, peacocks, and boats also which function as a selfie point.

One day Sia took Raghav to the park and while he was playing, another boy of his age or slightly older came close to him. He also wanted to climb the same stairs as Raghav while both were at the first step only. He pushed Raghav as he wanted to go first. Raghav fell on the ground. Luckily, he already had one foot on ground, so it was not a major fall. There was no injury as such. It was just the jerk that shocked Raghav and he started crying loudly. All of this happened in just few seconds. Before Sia could react and stop, it just happened. The mother of the other kid was far away talking on phone and has left the kid to roam around with no supervision.

Sia immediately took Raghav in her arms, dusted the dirt from his hands and clothes and started inspecting where he has got hurt. She was deeply stressed with the incidence as it was first time that it has happened. She was extremely worried. When she saw that there was no injury, she felt much better.

It was then that she focussed her attention on the other boy and started scolding him politely without raising her voice much. Why did you push him? Don't you have any manners? Where are your parents? By then mother of that kid realized that something has happened and hence she came running. Although Sia being just a teenager, she started scolding the mother instantly saying, "you should keep an eye on the child" and "see what he has done to my brother." Thankfully, the mother was a sensible lady and not someone who argues. Nowadays even if it is one's fault, they end up shouting at the other and blaming the other. She did not do that and accepted the mistake of her son and softly scolded him and left.

This reminded Sia of an old incidence when his father was in the same situation. Some other children had hurt her, and her father was furious. He is so possessive of his daughter that he even raised his hands to beat the other child. There was reddishness in his eyes out of anger and he was shaking. As he was about to beat the child, Sia stopped him to ensure the matter does not escalate. Upon watching tears in Sia's eyes, her father yet again went to beat the child but Sia stopped him again. The parents of the other kid also started shouting and quarrelling. Sia held her fathers' hand and dragged him away from the scene. Everyone around started staring and an entire scene was created. Sia's father was shouting and in return they were also shouting. Finally, it ended when Sia took her father away. She felt both good and bad at the same time. Good that how her father fought for her but bad because a quarrel happened. She thought her father should not have raised hands or his voice and could have managed the situation much more politely.

Sia thought if her father were here then he would have done the same thing again. He would have slapped the child and scolded their parents which would have escalated the matter. She started imagining how she would have been stopping her father and taking him away just like she did earlier. But she also missed him as there was no one to fight for Raghav and she had to deal with the situation on her own like an adult. She was tired of being the adult every time and just wanted to rest behind the guardianship of her parents. She does not want to solve any more complex situations and just wants to relax. She now realizes how difficult it is to be an adult.

Trivia - When in trouble, kids remember their parents even more.

Lesson 17 –
Visit to a mall

Fed up with following the regular routine for almost 2 years now, Sia decided to break the shackles and expose the child to more of outside world so that he also starts to learn how to mingle with others. Same old routine of bathing, feeding, playing, going to park etc has now got too boring. Even Raghav has lost interest in the same. Sia cannot see the same excitement anymore in him. Baby wants something new all the time to feel good. It excites the baby and keep his interest levels high. That is why it is important to introduce new toys, unfamiliar places, and new people to the baby at regular intervals. This helps in the growth of the child as well.

The best place to break the monotony and which also has kids' specific activity area is a mall. Mall has everything that a parent and a kid wants. A big accessible area to run around, lot of lighting and attractive boards, a food court for introducing different cuisines to the kid, a kids play area with all the slides, trampoline, ball pool, drawing area and much more. A perfect place to unwind and heaven for kids specially first few times before a kid starts losing interest but that comes late and till that time your purpose of keeping the baby engaged is fulfilled.

Keeping all these thoughts in mind, Sia decided to take Raghav to a nearby famous mall of the city. Moving outside with a kid is not a simple task. It involves planning and a lot of packing. Yes, that is right! You just cannot get ready and leave. There is a kid involved. What if the kid feels hungry during travel, what if he spoils his clothes by spilling food or urinating, what if he feels to poo, what if his stomach starts aching. All these are quite common scenarios and parents need to be prepared for all such emergencies. Hence the planning and packing.

So Sia starts the process of packing while housekeeper is looking after the kid. She takes out the kids' bag and starts putting each item one by one as she remembers it. Firstly, she keeps diaper and wet wipes, milk bottle, milk powder, some fruits, box of makhana for munching, boiled sweet potato, khakhra, medicines, hand towel, an additional pair of clothes. Just feel the number of items required to be kept for just a day visit to the mall. They are not going outstation. Just a couple of km away and this is the list. Phewwww! Sia takes a sign of relief that after much thought she has kept all that is required and now she can go to the mall fully prepared and relaxed.

They both leave the house along with housekeeper. It is going to be first time for Raghav. They stepped out of the house, sat in the taxi, and left.

Raghav has already started observing the cars and people passing by from the car's window. He is also enjoying the atmosphere within the car exploring all the things inside. Sia must constantly watch him and make sure he does not fall or hit his head somewhere as the car picks speed or stops or bumper comes in. Raghav is super excited. Siting inside a car is very new to him and he just cannot control his emotions. Jumping around in joy and enthusiasm. He started getting a little cranky as well along with excitement. This was the signal for Sia that he has started feeling hungry and so she opened the bag she has packed very judiciously (feeling proud about her efficiency) and gave some makhana to him for munching.

A few moments later as they were approaching the mall, Sia smelt a very foul odour - a fart. She immediately checked Raghav's diaper and there you go. He has pooped. Raghav also confirmed by saying "potta kiya". He is 1 yr and 10 months old and can say several broken collections of words by now. Thankfully, mall in nearby. Sia decided to clean him up once they enter the mall and then will continue their enjoyment.

After reaching the mall they cleaned him up in the washroom. They were now all set to rock and roll. Sia decided to take him to the kids play area first as he was full of energy and that would the best place for him to release that energy. They reached the kids play area, bought the entry tickets. But one thing disappointed Sia. Socks are mandatory to wear while playing inside the area. She was completely unaware about it and the proud feeling that she had for diligently packing the baby's bag is now gone and filled with slight disappointment.

She then bought the pair of socks from them and went inside. It was like a heaven from Raghav. His eyes completely lit up and was just not able to control his excitement. He quickly snatched away from Sia's clutch and ran towards the slide. He climbed up the stairs as quickly as he can and then sat on the slide and came down all by himself. He is a big boy now. Sia is watching all this as a spectator standing at the bottom of the slide filled with happiness and contentment.

Trivia - When a child does things by himself and does not require your hand holding, parent feel both relaxed (as they do not need to do that job anymore) and happy (that their child is growing up now).

After sliding for few times, Raghav was done with slides and was looking for some new thing to play with. Sia then took him to the trampoline for jumping. There were already several kids jumping around which motivated him further. He started jumping and falling and immediately started enjoying it as well. He laughed loudly upon falling each time. He was having a fun day today. All this while Sia looked at him and enjoyed his fun just like a parent. What an adult this 1 yr and 7 months of parenting has made Sia. She has developed all those emotions of happiness, sadness, grief, regret, joy, finding happiness in kids happiness, love and care at such an early age.

It has already been an hour or so since Raghav is having the fun of his life when Sia realises that he must be hungry and its already lunch time so let us take him to the food court, make him eat something and then bring him back again to the play area. So, they took a break from play. Well, it was not so easy. It was hell of a task to take him out of that area as he just cannot imagine his life without this play area. He cried a lot. Sia tried to convince him that they will get back here shortly after having lunch. With much difficulty Sia managed to bring him out of that area and took him to nearby food court on the same floor of the mall.

Sia thought south Indian cuisine will be a safe option as it is nutritious, light, low on spices and all. So, she went and ordered a plain dosa and idli wada combo for herself and Raghav. This was the first time Raghav was going to taste idli-wada. Dosa, they have introduced earlier as well at home. Wada was hot so she cut a small piece and cooled it down by blowing some air from mouth. When it was warm enough for him to have, she gave it to him and waited anxiously for his reaction. Thankfully, he liked it and asked for more. This means the dish is approved by the kid and can be given later also as part of daily food. This is how gradually an added item is introduced to the child every day. Sia has very quickly learnt all the tricks of the trade.

After the disappointment at the play area entry when they said socks are mandatory, little did Sia know another disappointment is waiting for her which will be bigger than the last one. After having the entire wada Raghav was full and asked for his favourite water bottle from which he drinks water all the time even at home. Guess what she forgot to keep it. OMG!! If you go back and see the list of items packed by her, water bottle is missing. This happens a lot, making sure to keep everything important, you end up missing some of the basic items itself. This was reason enough for Raghav to start crying inconsolably. Sia realised her mistake, got disappointed and immediately came into disaster management mode by taking him in her arms and trying to console him by showing him various other food items that were on display in the food court.

Trivia - want to make the child stop crying, try distracting him.

This is exactly what Sia did. She roamed around with Raghav and showed him attractive displays. She also bought him a new water bottle and made him drink water in it. After all these efforts for around 15 mins Raghav finally calmed down.

This incident reminded Sia of how she shouted at her mother once when she forgot to keep an important book in her bag for school (yes, she was so spoilt that she did not even pack her own bags). She screamed at her mother that because of her teacher scolded her and she vowed to not talk to her mother. This incident made her realise how wrong she was, and she should not have behaved that way with her mother. It is human to make mistakes, and one should be forgiving.

Seems like life has planned to teach a lesson to Sia for her every past deed of hers one by one through various new incidences as if God is planning to clean all her past bad deeds by making her suffer comparable situation.

Lesson 18 –
New cycle on 2nd birthday

After the grand celebration of first birthday, Sia was planning for a much humbler celebration of second birthday amongst themselves only and no friends or outsiders. That means the celebration will be among three members only Sia, Raghav and the old housekeeper. She wanted to keep it a private event without any glamour. Instead, she wanted to focus on the gift. A big gift not in terms of size but in terms of impact. Something which he cannot stop liking or being excited about. It must be special and long lasting. Something which he insists on playing every day by himself without being asked to play on it.

Apart from the gift, one another thing which she wanted grand was the cake. Raghav loves cake. Sia once introduced Raghav to cake at a nearby bakery shop and from then there was no looking back. He demands a cake daily but obviously Sia cannot give him as it will be lot of sweet for him. He loves chocolate cake, so flavour is also decided.

One last thing that needs to be done is a theme-based decoration of the living area of the house for some nice photographs. Although it is going to be a private affair, but some basic decoration is still required. As Raghav is very enthusiastic about various animals of the jungle, Sia decided to go for jungle theme with images of all the animals pasted on the walls. Even the cake will have jungle decoration on it with Cat, monkey, elephant being the prominent ones as they are his favourites.

So, theme is decided, and cake is decided, now only gift is left. Sia does have an estimate about the gift. Many a times she has observed that Raghav gets excited and totally engrossed upon watching a tricycle. Yes, a tricycle. Seems a reasonable gift which fits from all perspectives. Will be used daily and Raghav will ask for it himself without being forced into it. It is a long-term gift which will last couple of years at least. It will make him move his legs hence he will end up doing some exercise which will be good for his overall development. Not too heavy on the pocket as well. Sia has a strong feeling that she has chosen the right gift. As she is not aware of any good cycle shops in the vicinity, so she decided to go for an online purchase. Everyday once all the daily activities of Raghav are complete and he goes to sleep, Sia will take her mobile and search for a good and durable cycle within the budget. She was astonished to see so many options. These days lot of options are available for every item online. Shortlist, she applied various filters like the budget, brand, review ratings, colour, parental control etc and finally shortlisted 2-3 cycles. She then finally selected one which is from a reputed brand. She has heard that name and in fact she herself has a cycle of that brand.

All set now. She has ordered for the cycle and cake. Have also asked a local shop for decoration.

Luckily, the delivery of the cycle will happen couple of days before the birthday. She will have to hide it for those 2 days as she wishes to give surprise on birthday.

Sia has also developed an inclination towards donation. It is because of the tsunami of happenings in her life that has made think in that direction which is a good thing. She thinks that so many things that she had to go through others should not. So, in whatever small way possible for a girl of her age she has started donating for the past 1 year. That is why she has ordered a big cake of more than a kg thinking of donating to poor children sitting outside the nearby temple. Three of them can have only limited amount of cake and even after keeping some cake reserved for Raghav in fridge for 1-2 days they will be left with a lot of cake. So, she will be donating it. Ever since Sia has started donating stuff, she has felt a lot better and happier. Also, situation has improved at home also with much less troubles. Seems like God is happy with her gesture and is giving back some happiness to her.

Trivia - Nothing gives more happiness than giving.

It is couple of days to birthday and the cycle has arrived. Luckily, it arrived when Raghav was sleeping so it was easy to hide it from him. Now it is time to wait anxiously for the birthday and keep it a secret till then. Sia is already wanting to show the gift to her brother as she is so excited about it. But she must control her emotions. Every couple of hours she goes to the place where she has hidden the gift, looks at the packed tricycle, feels proud and happy about it and then close the door of the room and goes back to her brother. It is all incredibly special for Sia and she just cannot control her happiness. She takes pride in doing all these stuff for her brother and making him happy.

Finally, today is Raghav's birthday and it is time to celebrate. So, the plan is firstly to take a bath and get ready by 9-9:30 am and visit the temple first to take the blessings of God. So, they got ready in a hurried fashion and all three went to the temple. There they prayed for Raghav and the overall well-being of their family. Panditji on watching the cute small kid gave him laddoo as prasad which he loved it.

They then went back home, collected the cake, and left again. Sia wanted to cut the cake with kids of an orphanage nearby and then distributing the cake to the kids there as well as to the kids outside the temple. All the places are nearby and at a walkable distance. They went to the orphanage. Sia has already had a conversation with the lady manager there who welcomed them and took them to a big hall. She asked Sia to place the cake on the table at the corner of the hall. Gradually all the kids started coming in and taking a seat on the floor of the hall. It all happened in such an organised manner. Seemed like it was a daily ritual for them, and they were trained on when and where they must sit. It all seemed so mechanical. Sia felt both happy and sad at the same time. Happy that these kids will be getting a cake to eat today which they do not get. But sad about their condition. Sia felt like them because although her parents where there in coma in the hospital however currently it is equivalent to not having a parent. They have been in hospital for almost 2 years now and all that Sia has now is hope that they will come back one day. But many a times this hope also gets shattered when she overthinks about it and feels like an orphan. Therefore, she can relate to the situation of these kids and can feel their pain.

Soon within 15 mins all the kids gathered and sat in their respective daily seats on the floor. The lady manager asked them to stand up, join hands and pray to God before having their breakfast along with the cake. They all sang a beautiful prayer in chorus while Sia, her brother and the old housekeeper were standing and listening. Sia already has few tears rolling down her eyes. She is trying to control them otherwise her brother will look at it and will start asking questions and will feel that her sister whom she calls mom is sad. As the prayer finished, all the kids took their seats. The manager then asked Sia to open the cake and start the cake cutting ceremony. They gave Raghav a wooden knife in his hand and Sia assisted him to blow the candles and cut the cake while everyone sang happy birthday song. It was a cute moment. The old housekeeper then took over and divided the cake into equal small pieces to be distributed to all the kids. Sia had also sponsored a breakfast box for all the kids. She gave the money to the orphanage, and they arranged for the breakfast box. The box had several snacks items which are famous amongst the kids like samosa, dhokla, chips, frooti and laddoo. Sia held Raghav in one hand and breakfast box in the other. All the kids approached her one by one in a line in a very organised manner. Sia then handed over the boxes to them making Raghav touch each box before giving as if he is giving it to the kids. Each kid after taking the box moved ahead to the next counter where the old housekeeper was standing to give a piece of cake to every kid on a paper plate. It was all very professionally managed. Soon everyone received their breakfast and cake and started eating it. Sia and others also had the same breakfast along with the kids. She gave small pieces of everything to Raghav also to taste. He also loved eating all the item specially the frooti, laddoo and cake all of them being sweet items. He just loves sweets.

While everyone was finishing their breakfast, Sia asked for permission to leave from the manager. She graciously agreed and thanked her for the wonderful breakfast and cake. She also asked Sia to wait and then in a loud voice asked all the kids to thank Sia and Raghav for the tasty breakfast. They all stood up and said "Thank you Didi" in one loud voice. It was too overwhelming for Sia who was already feeling like crying. She just being a teenager almost gave them blessings like an adult within her heart. She then waved her hand to say bye to all the kids and left the place along with her brother and housekeeper. They then distributed the remaining cake to the children outside the temple.

What a day! It felt so blissful and satisfying. Sia almost forgot that she has a surprise for her brother which she has been hiding for 2-3 days along with controlling herself of revealing it before time. The time she spent in the orphanage gave Sia such a divine feeling that was simply unmatched. She felt why did not she do it earlier. Somewhere inside her she promised to do It every birthday of Raghav going forward. From being a snob, spoilt child to finding happiness in giving, what a journey she has covered in these 2 years. Who would have thought that she will become a person like this. It was a dream of her parents to see Sia become such a beautiful person from inside.

It is time to reveal the gift! On reaching home, Sia asked her brother to play in the living area while she just comes in 5 mins. Sia went inside and brought the tricycle from behind so that Raghav could not see. She has already unwrapped it yesterday to make it easier for Raghav to immediately start using it. She slowly approached towards Raghav from behind making sure she does not collide the cycle with house furniture ending up making a noise and eventually Raghav noticing it. Finally, she made it to the living room and kept the cycle next to Raghav. As soon as he turned, he was absolutely delighted. He screamed "kykl" in his toddler accent referring to the cycle. He was laughing and smiling endlessly. It was an absolute joy to watch his reaction. He was not able to control himself. He was jumping, laughing, then sat on the cycle, held the handle, turned it left right taking a feel of it, confused why it is not moving ahead as if it will do so by itself. Then he came down, observed the cycle from other angles, examined every part by touching and feeling it. In the process he asked endless number of questions. He put his hands on one part of the cycle and then asks "yeh Kya Hai?", Sia answers, then pointing to a different part and again asking the same question.

This thing continued till all the parts of the cycle got exhausted and so did Sia answering all his questions.

He was initially more interested in knowing the cycle before he rides it like a professional racer examining his automobile. He then sat on the cycle and asked Sia to take him around. Sia gave him a ride around the entire house, then got tired and asked the housekeeper to do so, then she got tired and this cycle repeated. Only Raghav was the one who was still energetic while the other two on the verge of collapse. It has been quite a hectic day for them, going places, carrying Raghav everywhere, and then cycling him around.

Finally, Raghav also started yawning so they immediately fed him lunch and made him go to sleep. After so much of activity he immediately went to sleep with minimal effort.

Overall Sia felt it was a fulfilling day. She was lying next to his sleeping brother, with a small photo frame in her hands which she took from side table. It had the photo of her parents. She was talking to them without uttering a word. First, she asked them that hope she is fulfilling all her duties nicely. Then she promised to behave properly to them once they return. This promise Sia must have done thousands of times ever since her parents went to coma, thinking that this promise will bring them back. She then pointed the frame towards Raghav and showed them that their baby is sleeping as if they were on a video call. Sia is totally in another zone. Her love for her parents has increased to another level and the desire for their return is at its peak. Hope god listens to her prayers.

Lesson 19 – Learning cooking

A significant part of a mother's responsibility is to provide food to her family. A housekeeper or a father can also cook and provide food however a mother's handmade meal is something else. It has so much love and care in it that it makes the food even more divine. In Sia's case as well the old housekeeper usually takes care of preparing food and Sia looks after the kid. That is how they have divided responsibilities amongst themselves. It is simply astonishing to see that for the past 2 yrs and couple of months since Sia's parents are in coma, the old housekeeper has not taken any leaves. Not even a single leave. She realises the fact that in her absence it will be impossible for Sia to manage everything. So, she never took a holiday and stood by Sia all the time.

However, the dream run is now over and the old housekeeper informed Sia that due to a property dispute back in her village she will have to go on a leave for 1 week at least. She must solve the dispute being the eldest of all the siblings plus has to sign few documents. So, she just cannot avoid going. It is mandatory. Luckily, they have a month's time to plan things out as she must leave next month.

That night after making Raghav sleep, Sia was making an action plan in her mind on how to pass those days when housekeeper will not be there. The main concern was food. Rest everything, she can manage and most of the work she already does. She does not know much about cooking. She can just cut a few veggies and put them in a bread to make a club sandwich or she can make maggie or cold coffee. That is the maximum she can do in cooking. Now the first question is how it is even possible to cook food while managing baby simultaneously. Second question is if she somehow manages cooking and kid both, then can she learn all the dishes which Raghav eats and become comfortable at it in such a brief time. She can always order food from outside, but it will be too much of outside food for the small kid. Sia wants to avoid that. Additionally, from an emotional angle, she wanted to give Raghav the taste of food prepared by mother which has love and affection in it. In this case the mother will be Sia.

The old housekeeper did mention that it will be too overwhelming for Sia and that she should avoid cooking. However, if Sia still insists she is ready to teach her in this one month. They can switch roles where housekeeper will look after the kid and Sia will do cooking based on the maid's verbal instructions. Time to time the housekeeper can come in kitchen and check if everything is going fine or not. It seemed a viable option to Sia, and she was willing to go for it because she wanted to give Raghav home food plus food made by her own hand purely out of love.

Next day, Sia informed the housekeeper that the plan is on. She will try to make food, and housekeeper will look after Raghav. Housekeeper started with the easy part which was dal and rice. She asked Sia to wash the dal and rice in separate bowls and soak them in water for some time. She then showed her how to cook them by adding few masalas etc. It seemed straightforward to Sia, and she quickly grasped it. It was a good start and Sia was feeling confident that she can pull it off. She got carried away because the items involved were easy to cook and there was someone to guide. Real test will happen when she does it alone. With the dedication and conviction, she is showing, it seems highly probable that she can pull it off.

Days went by and each day Sia learnt to make many latest items with special focus on those which Raghav can eat. Whatever she learnt the day before she tried to do it single handedly the next day for practice. She behaved like an obedient student and housekeeper was finding it quite easy to teach her. She is an adaptive learner.

Twenty days have passed and now only a weeks' time is left before the housekeeper goes on leave. There are no added items left to learn and all that Sia needs to do now is to practice as much as possible. She kept her small diary with her where she has noted the process for every item to help in case she forgets the recipe. This last week, Sia has declared as a mock exam week where Sia will be preparing everything without any help. She has learnt how to prepare dal, rice, poha, upma, vermicelli, oats, and few easy veggies. The only thing she is not comfortable in is roti. She is finding it difficult to learn that and has decided to postpone it to later. If required she will order roti from outside and rest, she will make at home.

Housekeeper was happy with the progress and felt satisfied that in her absence Sia can cook comfortably. However, one challenge remained in front of them, how will she be able manage kitchen and baby both. The only way out it either hold the baby in one hand and prepare food from the other (which is really difficult for Sia, specially looking at her fragile body frame) and the second option is to make the baby sit in the kitchen slab on one side and cook on the other side (in this option there is danger of baby touching a knife or other utensils and getting hurt).

Housekeeper insisted that it will be difficult and Sia shall manage food from outside from a hygienic restaurant. However, Sia was adamant. She had to cook. Sia then produced a game changing idea. She had a baby carrier in which she can hang the baby in front like a kangaroo. While the housekeeper was still there Sia quickly brought the carrier and assessed it on the spot. She put Raghav in it and wore in in front of her and then tried to do kitchen work. Raghav did feel uncomfortable at the start and tried to come out of it. Sia then left the kitchen work and roamed around the house singing a song while carrying him like a kangaroo. He liked it and gradually felt comfortable with it. This way he became used to of the carrier. Sia then again tried cooking while keeping him hanging in front of her. Although Raghav was comfortable now, but Sia was not as it was working as an obstacle, and she was not able to work. Then she wore the carrier the other way round by keeping him behind. Raghav also liked it and Sia was also comfortable. This way they finalized the position and solved this puzzle. Now

Sia is ready to cook and manage baby simultaneously. It was Sia's determination that all of this was being tried otherwise it was simple to order food from outside. Sia has become a typical freaky mother who is extra cautious for her kid.

In the last week with housekeeper, Sia cooked several snacks type meals and not the complete lunch and dinner. Her focus was Raghav's meal. If she is hungry, she can always order from outside. Sometimes she cooked with Raghav at her bag in that carrier or sometimes without him. Both ways she did sufficient practice and is now comfortable. As far as Raghav is concerned many a times, he rejected the snack prepared by Sia as it was not cooked properly or was missing certain ingredient. Very few times did Sia hit jackpot when Raghav really liked her dish and ate it completely. One out of four meals Raghav accepted, that was an incredibly low hit rate. So, although Sia might have become comfortable in cooking few items, but will Raghav have it or not that question remains. All depends upon Sia's accuracy. Sia promised herself that she will give her 100% and follow the recipe to the core.

Finally, the housekeeper left for her village with a promise to return after a week if not sooner. Sia was all on her own. The real test begins. She followed the daily routine as is - making Raghav brush teeth, bathe him, play with him, take him to park etc. In the morning after he was ready, Sia took him into the kitchen and made some sweet oats quickly. It was a quick one in which not much effort was required. Taking god's name, she gave Raghav the first bite of oats to eat. He took it in his mouth and made some faces. He then opened his mouth as if he were going to vomit. Sia was about to get heart failure. It was the first meal she made without housekeeper, and he is going to vomit. What will happen now? What will I give him to eat? All such question started coming in her mind. Surprisingly, he was just teasing Sia and immediately afterwards he closed his mouth and ate the oats. He then asked for more as well. Sia took a sigh of relief. It worked. He finished the entire oats. First meal completed successfully.

Everything went well for the next couple of days however testing time came on the third day. Sia was feeding Raghav some dal rice in lunch, and he was just not accepting it. He was moving his head away as soon as Sia brought the bite close to his mouth. When she insisted couple of times, he started crying. He was hungry that was sure as he had not had a meal in a while. He likes dal rice so that was also not an issue. Sia was wondering why he is not eating. He went on crying endlessly and gave Sia a nightmare. He was throwing away the food, crying on top of his voice making Sia go crazy. It was getting very messy and unbearable. Sia slapped the dal rice plate on the table in irritation and shouted at Raghav to stop crying. On getting scolded he started crying louder. Sia put him on the floor and started crying in frustration. So eventually both were crying with no solution in sight. It was an ugly situation. As always Sia had to ignore her emotions and behave maturely. She took few minutes, stopped crying, washed her face, and then gave another attempt at pacifying her brother. She then thought of tasting the food once to check what is the issue. She then realised there was no salt in it. She forgot. This must be the reason he is not having it. She then immediately added salt to it, gave him some love to calm him down and slowly tried to feed him again. After rejection for couple of times, he finally accepted the meal. Sia felt relaxed. After all the mess, target was achieved.

This event made Sia recall something similar from her past. She behaved exactly like this with her mother regarding the taste of food. That day Sia's mother made pasta specially for her as it is her favourite. Her mother served her pasta when she came back from school. She was overly excited about it. But as soon as she ate the first bite, she vomited it and shouted at her mother that it is so tasteless what have you made? You do not know anything? I hate you! And then entered her room and banged the door on her mother's face. Her mother felt bad and started crying but did not say anything to Sia. By chance, her father was also at home that day. He saw all of this. He pacified Radha (Sia's mother). Then he tasted the food and let her wife know that if she adds some more sauce and spices to it then it will taste better. She immediately did that and now it tasted good. She then knocked Sia's room door and asked her to have pasta now that she has corrected the taste. She did not open the door. After lot of convincing and father also coming into picture, she opened the door (mainly because of her father's insistence). She started having pasta making an angry face. But then she liked it, and her face changed to normal. Also, since she was hungry that is why she was showing more irritation. Once she ate all the pasta, she went into her room and slept. She did not even say sorry or thank you to her mother. She did not even feel a hint of guilt for her behaviour.

In the evening, her father had a word with her and told her politely that she should not have talked like this to her mother and asked her to say sorry. She understood her mistake and said sorry to mom and hugged her.

The same incidence happened with her today when Raghav did not have lunch. She got a taste of how a mother feels when her child does not have food which she has prepared with so much love and affection. She started crying after recalling that old event. She said sorry to her mom once again in her heart. She also apologized to God for her previous behaviour. Life is hell bent on teaching Sia a lesson the hard way.

Lesson 20 – Never say No

Sia noticed one thing between her parents that Dad mostly stays silent and does not say No to anything which she asks for while her mom used to stop and question her a lot on everything. This was a consistent trend. When she discussed it with her friends it was the case in their house as well. May be this is how male, and females are wired. Dads are cooler and silent while moms are more cautious and watchful. Naturally, she disliked her mom for this and loved her dad for agreeing to majority of her demands or requests. He has rarely said No and that too because it was not in Sia's benefit to do that. On the contrary, her mother acts like an investigative officer all the time trying to find out every detail about what Sia asks for. This annoyed Sia to the core. That is why most of the time she directly asked dad for permission. If it will not hamper his daughter's health, well-being, and safety, he is least bothered.

As Raghav grew and became more than 2 yrs old, he started doing variety of stuff which had to be monitored. Jumping on the sofa, touching the utensils kept on kitchen platform, running around carelessly, pulling the mobile charging wires, drawing with crayons on the walls, jumping on muddy potholes on the road and so on. A lot of it can result in he getting hurt if not monitored plus damage to household items leading to loss.

Sia had two options in front of her in such situations. She let him do whatever he wants but under supervision so that he does not harms himself. This way Raghav will love Sia as he is allowed to do everything. On the other hand, Sia can be very possessive and extra cautious and not let him have any fun and stop him from doing any such activities under the guise of protecting him from injuries. This way he would hate Sia.

Upon thinking about both the options, Sia recalled that one approach matches her father's approach while the other resembles her mother's approach. Now she is standing at that junction where she must decide which way she wants to take. In her heart she knows that she loved her dad because of his approach. So, she is inclined towards that approach. However, her inbuilt possessiveness towards Raghav is making her monitor closely every activity of his and stopping him every time thinking that he will hurt himself. So, she wants to be like her dad but naturally becoming like her mom. She now gets it what thought process her mother had. She now realises it was out of care and possessiveness and not because of anything else. She felt so embarrassed as she hated her mom for that and now, she herself is doing the same thing.

She finally decided that she will control her emotions and let Raghav do all kinds of activities that he likes while keeping a close watch on him. This way he can play in mud, throw stuff, and do whatever he likes with little interference from Sia. She will just stop him when he might hurt himself or about to destroy something valuable. She will be polite while stopping him and try to explain why she is doing that so that he learns the importance of things. This way he will not cry and get to know which items he can touch and what activities he can do.

Yet another learning for Sia that it is quite easy to criticize parents for everything. You do not think that they are making those decisions for your welfare. You think that they are trying to control your life and cage you. At that time, they are your enemies. However, when you are put in the shoes of your parents you also end up taking the exact same decision for your juniors and it is then you realize what is the thought behind it. There is only one thought and that is the welfare of the child and nothing else.

Till the time parents are making decisions and you are just required to follow them you feel life is simple but with no freedom. However, when you get the control to make decisions, it is then that you start thinking from all angles and realize that parents took the right decision. That is how life is.

Lesson 21 –
Finding bliss in Kids happiness

Post 2yrs+ of overwhelming stress of parenting, Sia would mostly be grumpy and irritated. She forgot how to enjoy and have fun in life. The burden was too much for her tender age.

One day while Raghav was sleeping, she was reflecting upon herself and thinking whether there is anything right now in her life that can make her feel good and happy. She tried hard to produce something. She then realised that the only time she is happy is when Raghav smiles, laughs, plays around cheerfully in excitement. So, in short, her happiness is now dependent on the kid's happiness. This is again a typical phenomenon in case of parents. They tend to lose interest in other worldly desires and find solace in their kids. Sia was experiencing it incredibly early in her life thanks to her situation.

She then started finding ways to give happiness to Raghav because she thoroughly enjoyed doing that. Raghav is very fond of toys. So Sia made sure she bought him new toys every few days. Whenever they pass through the toy shop on their way to the park, they stopped there for a moment. Raghav would then examine and look around to witness the world of toys. It was as if he has come to a fairy tale world. His excitement is beyond words. He would jump around trying to grasp every toy. What Sia did was every now and then she would buy him a toy which he selects making sure that it is not too costly and all. This way mostly he gets what he wants and both felt happy.

He is very fond of sitting in an autorickshaw. He just loves it. So, one day Sia bought him a toy autorickshaw. It was worth looking at the happiness on his face. On another day, she bought him a plastic bat and ball which he uses all the time. He already has tons of toy cars which he clutches on through the day and while sleeping. This way he has a vast collection of toys and Sia feels proud about it. She not only did it because of happiness for both but for one more important and priceless reason.

It is because she still remembers how her father pampered her with every doll and toy in the world. She was obsessed with dolls and her father made sure she had all the newly launched dolls even if it requires to be bought from foreign. Such was his love for her daughter. Sia still remembers all of it and deeply misses those days when she used to go with her father to the toy shop and buy dolls. She misses her father a lot. Losing a parent is a big loss. With the current situation she does not know if they will come back or not so at times, she feels that she has lost them.

She now realizes whether it is about buying a toy or taking an important life decision, how important are parents. Their presence itself is more than enough. You learn a lot from observing them and feel a confident and secure under their guidance.

Lesson 22 – Potty Training

One of the ugliest parts of parenting is cleaning the baby's shit. It is absolutely disgusting. Mostly it is the first time any person is introduced to cleaning someone else's shit. With the baby not cooperating and moving around it becomes even more difficult. At times it can be extremely smelly invoking a vomit in the caretaker. It instantly triggers a feeling in the mind of caretaker that my parents must have done it in my case just like every other parent. It makes you think how much a parent has gone through in bringing you up.

At first Sia found it impossible. She was not prepared for this. But she had no option. With cloth wrapped around her nose and wearing disposable gloves she started cleaning shit of Raghav along with assistance from the old housekeeper. She even cried many times as well while cleaning. It is because what life has made him do in her teenage. Gradually as days passed by and she became a professional babysitter, she started cleaning without gloves and all.

She once again apologized to her parents in her heart for being so tough on them. Just imagine how an activity like cleaning shit brings so much of emotions. It makes you realize how much parents have done for you and have never complained about it. They never even make you realize that they had to go through all of this. They always present good and happy things in front of you so that you do not feel depressed. They hide all their problems. On the other hand, the kid not realizing their sacrifice, keeps highlighting what is not there in his life or what all things his parents failed to provide as if it is their birth right. They never show gratitude to their parents for what they have. A part of it can also be because they are not at all familiar with the concept of gratitude, humbleness, kindness etc which comes with age unless explicitly taught. But at least they can give love and respect to their parents when they see them working so hard daily to manage everything. That is also missing. No respect no loves no affection and only cribbing. Someone needs to teach this to kids in an innovative way such that it remains with them forever.

To be honest, the ancient tradition of respecting parents, gurus and elders which is depicted in Ramayana and Mahabharata should still be followed and not alienated from our culture. No need to copy the way it was done in that era but at least the core values can still be retained.

Coming back to Sia, with months of cleaning shit, Sia thought that is it is the right time to train his brother to do potty in toilet with his baby toilet seat on the commode. Thankfully, he has started saying that he wants to do potty before doing it in his pants. Hence, it is easier for Sia now. She then immediately takes Raghav to the toilet and makes him sit on the seat. Many a times he faked, saying that he does not want to do any more and then later does in pants or other times he says it has done but does nothing. This way many times Sia had to clean him and his pants because he faked which irritated her to the core. So, after lot of iterations and pain, she achieved some success as Raghav stopped shitting in pants and always does it after removing his pants. But this success was incomplete as lot of times he used to do it in the room itself and not going to the toilet. So Sia had to clean the room but at least not the pants. Some progress. Then after even more iterations, Sia finally succeeded in her mission. He now does potty in the toilet only and nowhere else. A big relief for Sia specially after cleaning shit continuously for almost 2 years!

It is such a task to raise a child. Day after day of endless efforts. One milestone achieved, another waiting. There is no end to it. As some seasoned parents say it is a lifelong project. Even when the children become adults of age 35-40 years still, they share their problems with parents who are in their seventies and expect them to solve it. If the children have problem with their spouse or with their own children to whom will they share, it is only their old parents that they will share as sharing with friends and cousins is not a comfortable thing in most cases. The comfort level that is there with parents is unmatched. Noone can beat that. You can say your heart out and they will understand you. Still, we do not give them the due respect and love they deserve.

Lesson 23 – Nursery Admission

Time flies! Raghav is 2yr and 3 months old now. It has been complete 2 years now since Sia has been parenting him. OMG! When Sia looks back, what a transformational journey it has been. She is totally a different person now. Many of her old traits do not exist anymore. Even she has started disliking her old self. She does not even wish to remind herself about her old nature. All of it being positive changes which her parents wanted in her for so many years. Now when she is a changed person, her parents are not there to witness and experience it. What an irony! On the contrary, it is because of their absence only that she has improved so much.

It is time for another change or let us say another milestone in their life. While Sia was researching for a good play school for her brother few months ago just so that he learns to socialize and mingle with other kids. This would improve his learning as well. Being in the same house with the same person, learning might get limited even after significant efforts by parents. It important for kid to go out and explore the world and observe other kids and learn from their surroundings. She did not find a good play school as such in the vicinity and just few months to go for proper schooling to start she decided to directly enrol him for nursery in a reputed school which is famous in the town. It was none other than her own school. The same school which she had to leave due to her circumstances. Little did she know that she will have to go for admission one day for her brother in the same school. She was always of the view that in few months' times her parents will be healthy, and they will look after everyone like before and then she can have her normal life again. But it has been 2 yrs now and no signs of their return. Good part is that their condition is stable and has not deteriorated. She has not lost hope at all and prays for their wellbeing every day. Hope is all she has now.

It was during her research of that time that she got to know admissions will open in November for next academic year for Nursery. It is November now and she checked online that admission is open now. So, she decided to fulfil yet another duty of getting the admission done as soon as possible. It being a famous school, seats might get filled quickly. But Sia being an alumni of the school should get a preference. Additionally due to her unique case of parents going to coma and she leaving school, everyone in the school remembers her by face be it principal or teachers or students. She is famous in school due to her life story. Although Sia is not planning to use it for getting admission or scholarship of any kind, however there are high chances that her brother's case will be treated especially due to the reasons above. It is natural and Sia cannot get away from it. Any which way it is in favour of Sia so nothing to worry about.

Sia books an appointment and leaves the house to visit the school for admission. On the way, as the school approaches, she starts feeling nostalgic. This was the same route she used to follow every day for school. It has been ages since she took this route. The taxi drops them on the gate of the school. As soon as Sia comes close to the main gate and watches the large banner displaying her schools name it becomes overwhelming. She feels like crying. Never ever in her wildest dreams did she thought that she will be coming to this school as a guardian and not as a student at such an immature age. Nobody would have thought that. It is a rare situation. She then starts walking inside the school with a tsunami of emotions flowing inside her. These were the same corridors where she used to run in uniform carelessly along with her friends. They used to play all sorts of games there. It was such a beautiful life. But it was god's wish to make her a guardian from a student at such an early age. Nobody is bigger than the will of God. Amongst all these emotions, there was also a small ray of happiness that if not her then at least her brother will live his school life the same way she did and was supposed to live if everything was fine.

Trivia - Oh my goodness no one knows what life has in store for them in future so live every moment happily.

She then entered the admission room where she saw the admin madam sitting. Madam recognised Sia immediately as she was the one who did all the exit formality for Sia when she decided to leave school. Madam hugged Sia and the baby and asked them to sit down. She then asked Sia how everything was going and is she doing well or not. Does she need any other help apart from admission. Madam could feel the emotions in Sia's eyes what she must be going through coming to school as a guardian and not student. She asked Sia to have some water and juice, keep her bag on the side and asked Raghav to play in the small kids play area right next to the admission section. So, Raghav got involved in drawing and other activities there. Meanwhile Sia and madam were doing casual conversation about what has changed in school since Sia left. Madam was a very empathetic person and made all efforts to make Sia comfortable. After a small conversation of 10-15 mins, she then briefed Sia about the admission procedure. She gave her a form to fill and make the necessary payments. Sia had already bought few documents like birth certificate etc which were required. After completion of all the formality and payment, madam confirmed that the admission is almost complete and just one formality is left. That formality is to meet the principal mam once. In other cases, without meeting principal admission is not confirmed but in Sia's case it was just a formality as principal mam already knows her and just want to meet her once as it has been long. They went to meet the principal; the guard asked them to wait for couple of minutes as she was finishing her other meeting.

Principal is free now and asked them to come in. The guard opened the door, and principal was sitting right in front. The principal was reading some document with her spectacles lying on the edge of her nose. She looked upwards by just moving up her eyeballs with her eyebrows sharply forming inverted V shape. Her head is still in the same position pointing towards the document on her table. She saw Sia was standing with Raghav in her arms. A smile came on her face on watching Sia and she gestured with her arms to come in and have a seat.

Sia sat down and let her brother stand next to her. He started twisting his body and looking at everything around in a playful manner while they started talking. The principal took couple of mins to finish reading the document and then took off her glasses and making a deep sigh welcomes Sia and asks how she has been all this while. Sia gave a summary of the last 2 years in a positive way and not trying to sound miserable. She wanted to give her best in front the principal and wanted to show her that everything was going well. The principal then asked Raghav what is your name? Raghav hesitated to reply and clinched on to Sia. Then Sia also insisted on telling his name. He then in a very weak voice said "Ragb" trying to say Raghav. Principal smiled and accepted his answer. She then asked few more questions to which Raghav gave some reply which a toddler gives. Principal was trying to judge Raghav's overall growth in terms of speech, grasping, motor skills etc through observation and questions. She seemed satisfied and gave her consent for admission without saying anything. Principal mentioned to Sia that she is looking forward to her joining back school whenever possible. She then gave a quick brief of activities that are done in Nursery and their teaching methods. They then said goodbye to each other and Sia left the principal's office along with Raghav.

Sia felt that the meeting went well and hence took a sigh of relief. She then went back to the admin madam. She was already talking on the school intercom phone with the principal. It was pretty evident that principal must have called to give her feedback. Madam then put the phone down, smiled at Sia and nodded her head in affirmation that admission is confirmed. Sia smiled and thanked her and shook her hands. They then left the school filled with positivity. Yet another milestone achieved by Sia as a guardian.

As she was walking back from the same corridors in return, she remembered attending parent teacher meeting with her parents and walking through the same corridors along with her parents. She remembered that most of the time while returning she used to complain to mom that why did you say this or that in front of the teacher etc. It was always a small quarrel while returning, because every time Sia had some complaints or the other with her mom regarding her conversation with the teachers. She was very conscious about her image and never liked if her image would get spoiled due to her mom's words or actions.

Today she is returning as a guardian and not as a student. She is at her mother's place and Raghav is at her place, the only difference being there is no quarrel as all of this is beyond Raghav's understanding. Sia thought that there can be a day few years later when he can also quarrel with her. Without any quarrel whatsoever Sia was already feeling bad thinking about the scenario when Raghav will do this to her. She felt very awkward and uncomfortable from even the thought of it. She then thought how her mother would have felt when she had to face all those quarrels. She felt very embarrassed on being so rude to her mother. Like always she apologized to her mom in her heart and promised she will never do it again if she gets another chance to live with her.

It is unbelievable how a simple corridor of a school can bring back so many memories and in Sia's case some regrets as well. She could only think of her bad behaviour towards her parents and can rarely remember anything positive when she made them smile. She is ashamed of herself. She is just not able to recall any positive or happy memories with them. All the memories are filled with rudeness, attitude, negativity, crying etc. What a bad child was she but still her parents never ever made her feel like that. That is why she is realizing all of it now in their absence.

Lesson 24

"Want the small Sia back again"

Madhav, Sia's father, always used to say she wants the old small and cutie pie Sia back again. Sia always wondered why her father says this every now and then. Initially she thought may be because she was cute and small back then, so her father wanted her of that size to play with her all over again. She tried to confirm this theory with her father, but he always gave a sarcastic smile and continued doing whatever work he was doing without saying anything. Never did he say yes or no to this reasoning from Sia. Neither did he explain properly what he meant by that. So Sia finally gave up, left it there and stopped thinking much about it.

It is after so many months of parenting and living without parents that Sia thinks she has finally got the answer to it. She strongly believes that this new reasoning is the right one. She realised that she became very rude to her parents of late and did not treat them with due respect. She took them for granted and many a times mistreated them. She misbehaved with them, threw unnecessary tantrums did not speak to them at all in case of any fights etc. Now when she looks back and analyses those events, she strongly feels that all of it was uncalled for. All of it could have been avoided and it was purely due to her attitude that it happened. Her parents purely out of their love for their daughter never retaliated and kept their anger and disappointment within themselves. They never showed their feelings to Sia, no matter how much she hurt them emotionally. After all she was their child, they loved her, ignored her mistakes and attitude, considering it to be a teenage factor. But due to this she was never able to realise her mistake as they never taught her a lesson or tutored her on this matter.

Now that she herself has done parenting and ignored countless mistakes and troubles created by Raghav, she now understands what it is to be a parent. She also does the same thing to Raghav and that too naturally. She never scolds him, ignores everything, and continues loving him. Parenting taught her to be like this.

Due to the innocence of this small age, the child never answers back rudely, does not show tantrums, and is closely bonded with their parents. Therefore, this phase of parenting gets strongly inscribed in their minds. They always recall this phase when a child grows up. They miss this phase as it was cute. They want the kid to be obedient and show the due respect and love to them because they love their child immensely and when the child reciprocates it is a wonderful feeling for parents. It was her bad behaviour which reminded her father of the small Sia who would always look for her father and play with him all the time. Who would cry when father left for office and would jump with joy when he returns. Those are the moments which a father misses a lot and that is why he says, "want my small kid back".

Sia has cracked this puzzle now and is almost sure about it. Just waiting to confirm it once with her father. She also promised her father that once he comes back, she will always be his small little cute Sia for life.

Chapter 5

The Moment has Arrived

It is February and Raghav have completed 2.5yrs of age. Day by day it is getting comfortable for Sia to manage her brother in many aspects. He informs before potty and does his business in toilet making it easier to clean and all. He can use a spoon to eat food and can also eat food comfortably from hand. He speaks proper 4–5-word sentences now clearly expressing what he wants making it quite easy for Sia to understand things unlike before where it was all about guessing and trial and error. He sleeps the entire night and does not wake up in the middle of the night. He can climb stairs and do fun rides in park all by himself with little or no assistance. Sia can spend some time with herself while he is occupied with some game or watching rhymes on tv. It is set now. Life has become stable for all of them. The initial months of chaos are now over and Sia and the old housekeeper can take a sigh of relief now. They just need to follow the schedule and that is it.

Sia can now spend some time on herself like going to parlour for haircut, talking to friends, watching some series on OTT etc. She has now started to socialize as well. She leaves the kid behind with housekeeper and goes to meet few of her friends nearby. All this is possible because things are settled now and everyone else has accepted Sia's situation and does not give her any more advice or suggestion. They just appreciate the effort that Sia has put in.

They are not even aware of how far Sia has come in terms of her personality. She has become a girl full of grace from all aspects. It is pretty evident to her friends and family members of friends when she goes to meet them. Her conduct has totally changed. Earlier she was full of attitude and did not properly greet friends' parents when she visited their house and used to just run towards her friend's room. Now as soon as she enters her friend's house, she first greets their parents properly, take their blessings by touching their feet, spends some time talking to them and then goes to friends' room and that too after asking permission. Upon leaving she inform the parents that she is leaving and if she is leaving along with her friend then informs the parents by when they will be back home. She has become very humble, talks politely, always smiling, is happy and content with what she has and has no signs of greed or want. Unbelievable. What a change! This is god's magic. Krishna Leela as they call it. Only he can bring such a change in a human. Sia must be the chosen one whom God wanted to become a better person. Not everyone gets that chance. Although the process of making her such graceful girl was full of sadness and pain, but the output is purely gold.

God still has some more situations for Sia to face. He is not done yet. It is something for Sia's betterment only because he knows the best. Now that everything was going stable suddenly a shocker comes. Sia gets a phone call from hospital. They asked her to come to hospital immediately as her parents condition was deteriorating. The phone slipped from her hands, and she started crying endlessly. Watching her Raghav also started crying. The old housekeeper tried to console both and asked Sia what is the matter. She did not reply and just kept on crying. After collecting herself and much insistence of housekeeper, she said that parents are not well, and she needs to go. Housekeeper said do not worry she will take care of everything here and asked her to leave for hospital immediately. As it could be her last meeting with parents, she was in a dilemma whether to take Raghav with her or not. Watching such things is not good for a child. But at the same time if it is the last time, then at least he should see his parents once. Sia was not in a state to take any decision. Her brain was frozen. She was just not able to process things around her. Upon realising Sia's situation, the housekeeper thought it would not be correct to leave Sia alone, so she went along with them to the hospital. It was the housekeeper only who packed the bag for Raghav, booked taxi and took them to hospital. She had to hold both Sia and Raghav as she was not in her senses. She was absolutely lost and crying all the time. That one hope she had all these years is now shattered. The thought that She is going to lose her parents is not letting her stop crying. She has felt this feeling of losing them thousand times in the past couple of years but still that phone call from hospital was too terrifying.

Somehow, they reached the hospital. Sia must be brave and face the situation. She tried to gather herself, washed her face with cold water and then went to the room. She saw hurried activity in the room with doctors and nurses monitoring everything on urgency, they are running in and out of the room taking blood samples, giving injections etc. It was even more terrifying. One senior doctor on watching Sia, came towards her and took her to his chamber. He then briefed Sia about the condition of her parents. He said that her mother was still stable, but her father blood pressure has dropped and is not responding to injections. They are planning to give him high dosage of steroids to boost the functioning and then will keep him under observation. Anything can happen now, and everything is based on his willingness and determination to live. Sia started crying again after listening to all of this. Doctor knew it was going to be hard, but he must do his job of letting the family member know of the latest updates. Doctor them left for examination and Sia and housekeeper sat outside the room. Housekeeper was trying to console Sia. Sia then realised that there is only one way to instil hope in the situation and bring her father back and that is by praying to God. She started her prayers, chanting the name of God and reciting few mantras wish she has learned in the recent past. She asked the housekeeper to look after Raghav and show him his parents, make him touch their feet and take blessings while she was praying outside. Sia then did not stop for a moment and kept on praying tirelessly. She was hell bent on giving a tough fight to whatever God throws at her. She is a strong girl now. She has realised that she is already living a life without parents at home for couple of years now. What more could change. It is only that her parents will leave the hospital and live with God in heaven. That is the only change that will happen. Rest all will remain same as it was in the recent past. By now she has already learnt many things that an adult does and will keep on learning new things to manage life of her and her brother.

She continued her prayers while all such troubling thoughts came into her mind. She decided that she will not leave this place where she was sitting till, she gets the next update from the doctor. She asked the housekeeper to leave for home with Raghav as it was too much for him. He did not want to leave Sia and was crying but housekeeper took her away. Right now, Sia's only priority was to pray. She has become numb, none of her senses were working properly. She was blank. She sat on the chair outside the room, head down and kept praying. After a long wait of 3 hours when the sun was about to set, doctor called her inside the room where her parents were. She was highly terrified. The decisive moment has arrived. She has never felt like this before. None of the examination result stress or parenting stress come close to this. That is the maximum stress she has taken till now. She stood up and went inside. Doctor was standing next to her father. He asked to come close and stand next to him. He put his hands on her head to comfort her and said "Relax! He is out of danger." OMG! She immediately fell on the ground and started crying with her hand on her mouth, but this time in happiness. God has listened to her prayers. This was her toughest test so far. Doctor held her and made her stand again, gave her some water to drink and hugged her to give some comfort. He then asked her to spend some time with her father and then leave for home as it was getting late. Everything is fine and no need to worry. All of them left the room. Now she was alone with her parents. She almost shouted at her father for scaring her. She scolded her father and asked him not to do it again. She then hugged him and her mother and kissed them. After spending some more time with them and talking whatever random things that came in her mind, she left for home promising to come again tomorrow to meet them.

What a day it was. She will never forget it. She is still wondering what wrong she has done for which she is facing so many troubles in life. Upon reaching home, she was so drained and exhausted that she asked housekeeper to stay back tonight and sleep with Raghav while she went in her bedroom and crashed to sleep immediately. How is it to lose a parent, she felt it very closely today. It is the most terrible feeling on earth. Something which you can never reverse. All your remaining life you must live with that pain. Nothing can take away that pain not even time. No matter how old you grow, you will still miss your parents. There are old people of 60-70 years of age who can be seen crying while remembering their parents. It is the ultimate loss. A loss from which one can never recover. They can just continue living their life with that inherit feeling of pain and disappointment that they could have done so much more for their parents if they had more time. They had so many more things to talk about. So much to live and experience together which will never happen now. Full of regrets and guilt it is. Life is never the same post losing a parent. You are not the same person anymore. A part of you is dead. You are just living to provide for your loved ones. Nothing in the world excites you now.

What to do. That is how life is. Everyone who is born is destined to die. One should accept the fact and live the rest of the life, properly and do not go into depression. It would be a great disrespect to God if you live the rest of your life in depression and adopting bad habits. That is not the right way. You must deal with it in a positive way. Learn to manage the pain and continue performing your duties. You brought nothing and will not take anything when you die. That is the law of the land. Accept it and move forward.

Chapter 6

Parents Return or Farewell?

The last incidence where Sia's father blood pressure dropped, and chances of survival were 50:50 that incidence shook Sia to the core. Ever since that incidence she cannot get a relaxing sleep. She is always scared after then. Scared of every phone call that comes. Scared of every visitor that comes home. Just like a family member of a soldier serving for the country on the border are always tensed of receiving phone calls from authorities or a military personal visiting home. It is such a traumatic experience for a family member. Sia can now understand the feelings of family members of a soldier. Her situation is the same.

Raghav is now 2.5 yr old. He has achieved all his milestones till now and his growth is good as per doctor. All his vaccination is also up to date. Everything is going fine except for parents who are still lying in coma. Amongst all the events in the past 2.5-3 yrs, one event was given the least amount of importance and that was Sia's birthday. Everyone was so engrossed in taking care of the child and settling life overall that Sia's birthday went on back burner. Sia was fourteen when she started parenting, when her 15th birthday came in February it was only due to WhatsApp messages and calls did, she recalled that it was her birthday. What an irony!

She was a type of girl who used to plan for her birthday months in advance. And look at her now, forgetting her own birthday was unbelievable. This is what parenting does to you. Nothing else remains important. It is only the wellbeing of your child which is important rest all does not matter. You are so engrossed in taking care of the child that what is going on around you, does not have any impact on you. There can be big financial or political events happening in the country and your nearby surroundings, but you are least bothered. You are not even aware of those events. All you are aware of is whether your child has eaten or not, whether he is doing well or not etc. Starting couple of years are too demanding. For a teenager like Sia it was even more a daunting task. So Sia completely forgot her 15th birthday.

Second year of parenting is still lighter as compared to first, so this time Sia did remember that it is her birthday but did not want to celebrate it.

Next year in February when she turned sixteen, the old housekeeper remembered her birthday and tried to make something special for her to eat on that day. Sia took a small piece of the desert she made as a token of respect for the old housekeeper and asked her to give the rest to Raghav and to poor kids outside temple. The old housekeeper understood that she is in no mood to celebrate and respected her decision.

Today after 2.5 years of parenting, her 17th birthday is approaching and is just round the corner. She is hell bent to celebrate it with parents and ready to fight with God to any extent for that. She is done living without parents. She understands all the lessons which God wanted to teach her to make her a better person. She acknowledges that and has shown improvement also just like the way God wanted. So she is of the view that since she has done her part by living though the challenges that God gave in her life and made meaningful improvements in her then now it is God's turn to give her return gift by bringing her parents back to life just like before. No doubt Sia's thought was in the right direction and her demand was also genuine. Now it is on God whether he listens to her or has more challenges planned for her.

She has decided that she will take the cake to the hospital room where her parents are and will cut it there only. If God is kind and heals her parents before that then nothing like it else if they are in this same condition, then she will still celebrate with them. She will make them wear the conical birthday cap, she will play an old video of them singing happy birthday for Sia, she will hold their hands and collectively cut the cake. Basically, involving them to the fullest. This is her way of telling herself that they are with her and have not gone anywhere. This is a direct one on one strong message to God that enough is enough I want my parents back. It is not that she is not able to manage her brother or the house without them. It is just that she wants then back desperately. She has now realised their worth completely and do not want to lose that treasure of love, affection, care, and support. She is feeling vulnerable and needs a hand of elder on her shoulder. She is not at all making any unnecessary demands. She has earned that by dedicating her past couple of years on her brother and herself. She deserves it. But does God also think likewise or has another plan. Only he knows.

Just like Raghav's birthday she ordered cake from the same shop. The cute thing being she does not order cake of her choice, instead she ordered a fruit cake which both of her parents loved.

This again goes to show that she has matured to think of others around her and not just being self-centred. She can now sense what others are feeling from their words and behaviour. She then acts accordingly to make them feel comfortable. All these are signs of maturity which one gets late in life however Sia got it in her teens only. She is lucky in that aspect. She also ordered the birthday cap. Yet another cute thing she did was she wore a beautiful red dress which her father bought her from abroad when he went there for business meeting. She absolutely loved the dress and hugged her father tightly that day. Again, she is not wearing that dress because she likes it but instead because her father chose it for her. Because it is her father's choice. If at all he opens his eyes, he will see her in that same beautiful dress which he chose. Yet another sign of being considerate and putting family members liking ahead of hers. Such a beautiful person she has become. They will be genuinely proud of her. She also decided to carry a sling bag which her mother gifted along with her favourite perfume to make her feel that she is carrying stuff which she has gifted also and not only the ones gifted by her father. This was something special. She is leaving no stones unturned here. Taking care of every minute details so that none of her parents feel left out as if they are in conscious state. Because in Sia's mind they are back into consciousness, and they are with her. There is absolutely no doubt about that in her mind. Such was her level of confidence.

The day has arrived. Sia asks the housekeeper to give Raghav a bath while she gets ready as today, she will take some time to dress. She took a bath and then straight away went to the mandir room and prayed for an hour chanting mantras, reading hanuman chalisa and sundar kand. Like her father she was also a strong believer of Lord Hanuman. She does not pray for such long. Today being her birthday, she wanted to pray longer, so that she gets the blessings of God and let him know that she is a changed girl and remind him about the gift she has asked for. Praying also gives positivity which she wanted in abundance specially today when she will be celebrating birthday with parents after a gap of 2.5 years. She is consciously making all the right moves from starting of the day as if she has it all planned in her mind.

She then goes to see what Raghav is doing. He was already in his new clothes which Sia bought for him yesterday and has also had his breakfast. They then packed the bags keeping all the necessary belongings and whatever they need to celebrate birthday in hospital. After checking all the items, they then left for hospital. As they were approaching the hospital, anxiety levels started rising within Sia. She just could not understand why she is feeling so anxious. Her voice was shaky, her body movements were jittery, it was as if she was going to see her exam results. She was unable to understand why she is feeling like this when she is going just to celebrate a birthday in a very private fashion. There was a hint of excitement as well in that anxiety. It was totally a different feeling which she has not felt earlier. She has become used to such things now, where she feels all sorts of emotions together, having gone through so many difficulties in life. She ignored this anxious feeling thinking it to be yet another strange feeling that keep on happening to her. She moved on as she had a bigger purpose ahead.

They went to the private room where her parents were resting. Sia informed the nurses that they will be doing a small celebration without making much noise. Nurses understood the occasion and happily gave their consent.

Sia then closed the door of the room, puts all the bags down on the side and immediately touches her parents' feet and gives both a tight hug one by one. A hint of tears can be seen in her eyes. It was an emotional moment for her. She then made Raghav also touch their feet and take blessings. In the room there were two single beds on which her parents were resting and there was a sizeable space in between the beds such that a person can put a chair and sit there along with a small table. This was enough for them to put the cake in that table in the centre of the two beds. Sia wanted to go slow and enjoy every moment. She first sat on a chair between the beds, took one hand of father in her one hand and in her another hand took her mother's hand. She held them tightly and brought both the hands close to her eyes and touched them to her forehead again trying to take their blessings and some warmth of their love. She then held their hands in front of her eyes with her head down and started crying. She tried to keep it subtle to not make Raghav cry, but she could not control her tears.

Tears from each of her eye dropped on her father's and mother's hand. THEIR HAND VIBRATED! OMG! What just happened. Are they back to consciousness? Is her wish fulfilled by God? Before she could get happier, she realised that the door of the room was opened by a nurse and the vibration could be of that as well. It was an old building so as soon as the door or window opens slight vibration can be felt. She thought that God is still not in a mood to give her some happiness of having a family. Nurse came to take one of her belongings which she accidentally left in the room and then left.

Anyways after that false alarm, Sia continued with her celebration. She opened the cake and put it on the centre table. She put the birthday cap on her parents' head. She put the mobile phone on a stand and started the old video of her parents singing. She then again held both their hands like she was holding few minutes ago along with a wooden knife. She blew the candles and cut the cake. It was as if they were holding the hands of Sia while she was cutting the cake just like they used to do in good old days. All this while, their own voice singing happy birthday was playing in the background. This way Sia involved all their senses in this celebration no matter if they were working or not. She was determined to do so, and she did. Holding their hands while cutting cake (touch), making them listen to their own voice singing a song (hear), she applied some cake on their lips (taste) as she did not want to do anything stupid and make them sicker, she wore their favourite perfume (smell) all these four senses got involved. Only the fifth sense of sight cannot be applied as their eyes were closed.

Still, it was a great attempt to have even thought of it in such a scientific way. None would have thought like that. It was a very smart move from Sia. All credit goes to her mastermind planning.

After applying cake on their lips, she then gave cake to Raghav and the housekeeper with her own hands. Housekeeper also gave Sia some cake to eat. Raghav was in love with the cake and asked for more continuously. They had to hide the cake and act like it was finished to make him stop asking for more. He absolutely went crazy. This added some playful fun to the celebration. After having cake and other snacks which they brought they just sat down and relaxed. Sia was sitting on a chair in the middle of the beds while housekeeper and Raghav were sitting on a small cot at the corner of the room meant for visitors. There was a small TV as well in the room which they thought of opening so that Raghav can see some cartoon to keep him busy. Sia started the TV and as she was flipping through the channels she heard some beeping sound. She thought it must be from the TV and ignored it and continued flipping to reach to the cartoon channel. As soon as she reached the cartoon channel the beep sound intensified. She then realised that it was not from TV but from the medical device which monitors their vital parameters. It was coming from both the machines father's as well as mother's. Sia panicked. She thought it is something like last time when she almost lost her father. Is it because she applied some cake on their lips, and it has reacted to any medicines? Is it because she accidently did something with the machines while celebrating? She started questioning her own act and blaming herself for all of it. Looking at Sia, the housekeeper realised that she has panicked so she immediately took Raghav with her outside and informed the nurse about it. She remained outside with Raghav as a small child should not see all of this. Nurses immediately called the doctor available on duty and rushed to the room. They started checking the readings on the monitor, examining the machines etc while doctor was coming. Only the doctor can tell what is happening. They asked Sia to leave the room as it will make her panic more. The doctor arrived and they closed the door and started examining.

Sia was broken. She was cursing herself to have produced this idea of celebrating with parents. It was all her fault. She tapped her head from behind several times as if punishing herself. She was disgusted with herself. What was she thinking when she produced this idea. Does she know that her parents are critical and such things should be avoided. These are all after thoughts. Damage has been done. Now they must wait for what doctor says and can do nothing apart from feeling guilty. Sia was crying inconsolably. She was on the verge of losing her parents this time both and she could never forgive herself in her entire life. She will blame herself for her entire life. She has already started saying sorry to God and requested God to forgive her and do not take her parents away from her. She is totally broken.

After an hour of examination and several in and out of the room by the doctors, Sia was called inside.

It was yet another decisive moment for her. What is going to happen. Are they all waiting inside to give her the ultimate shocking news? Will she be able to bear this loss? All sorts of questions arose in her mind full of negativity. How can one think positive in such situations. With highest level of anxiety ever, shaky legs and shivering body she entered the room. There were several doctors and nurses standing there. Some of them were senior doctors and rest junior residents. She approached towards one of the senior doctors who have been supervising this case since starting. He asked her to come closer, partially hugged her from side to make her comfortable and said "You have done a MIRACLE. Your parents' senses are back". He then showed Sia their partially open eyes, slight movement in their heads and fingers. She immediately fell on the ground and started crying loudly. She just cannot believe it. Immediately an image of Lord Hanuman came in front of her eyes giving him the gift she wanted. Yes, God had no more plans to assess her. It is all done now. It is time to give her back what she truly deserves. She joined her hands and bowed down to Lord Hanuman. Her belief in God solidified forever. This was a miracle. How can they come to senses today and not earlier. Only God has the answer. Sia controlled her cry and was assisted outside by one of the nurses. Doctors asked them to go home for now as they need to do some more tests and give her proper report tomorrow. There was no need to wait as it will take the entire day for the investigation and report preparation. Sia was not at all willing to leave as she wanted to be with her parents whom she got after so long. But doctor asked her to let them do their job and wait for one more day where she has waited for years. Also, they could not talk yet so no point of being there with them. There is also a fear of coma relapsing if anything goes wrong. Keeping all this in mind Sia agreed to leave. She mentioned to the doctor that she will arrive early morning tomorrow as she just cannot wait. Doctor advised not to come too early and that they will call her to come, so no need to hurry. They can sense the excitement in Sia. And why it should not be there. It must be there. She has gone through a lot and wants her parents back.

Adhering to doctor's advice they left for home. Sia and the old housekeeper both were super excited. Their long-awaited wish is coming true. They have already started imagining them in normal condition, talking, walking, and eating just like a normal person. Their enthusiasm is beyond words. When Sia started parenting initially the only thing that was there in her mind always was when will she get her normal life back. She used to miss going to school, meeting friends, hanging around and every other thing that she did daily. She loved her life back then. From that to live a totally contrasting life was a humongous change for her. It was exceedingly difficult for her to accept and adjust with it. So, every time she thought when will God give her old life back. Gradually she learnt her life lesson and now more than getting her old life back Sia is excited to have her parents back. She is happy to continue parenting Raghav even after her parents are back. She just wants them back in her life. That is her only wish.

They are expecting too much of a difference from tomorrow itself. However, that might not be the case. It takes time for recovery after being in coma for so long. They may open their eyes and watch Sia and Raghav and the housekeeper. They might not remember them. They might remember but have lost speech so not able to communicate. Any and everything is possible right now. None of the possibilities can be negated. They are not prepared for such possibilities. They are assuming that everything will be like before and why not. They should be optimistic. However, anything can happen tomorrow. Doctors are performing all sorts of tests today to confirm the same.

Sia was not able to sleep all night. The excitement mixed with anxiety was at it extreme and unbearable. She practiced all night how will she greet her parents; what will she say to them? Shall she scold them out of love for being away for so long but that might affect them badly, so shall she touch their feet but that will be too formal. All such thoughts and scenarios raced through her mind the whole night. She kept on building different scenarios in mind and accepting or neglecting them. She practiced all night as if she were going to meet the Prime Minister. They were her own parents but still she wanted to be cautious of not making any mistakes which affects them adversely. She created top few scenarios in her mind and how I will she reacts in each of them. Throughout the night she perfected her response in those scenarios minute by minute as if she were writing a scene of a movie. It was the most difficult night for her. Controlling all those emotions were not easy at all. Who prepares so much for meeting their own parents. But this situation was unique and did require some amount of preparation just to ensure that she does not harm them through her actions as they are extremely vulnerable at this stage. All they need is love and care right now just like a small baby and nothing else. No negativity no mischief nothing.

Finally, the morning arrived with the sun shining bright. Daily routine kept Sia occupied and hence kept her anxiety under control. She was eagerly waiting for the call from hospital. She deliberately kept herself busy throughout the morning so that her attention remains diverted, and she does not think about her parents and how will she meet them. She did all the household chores even those which the housekeeper does so that she can pass more time.

It is already 10 AM and still no call from hospital. She has started feeling disappointed and wants to leave for hospital anyway. But she knows that they will not allow her to meet her parents so no point going there. She then went to the nearby temple along with Raghav and prayed to God. This was in addition to her regular prayer at home. Then went to the park which was adjacent to the temple and made Raghav do some rides and played with him. All the while in the park she was looking at her wristwatch and checking the time. Every minute was difficult to pass. She called an old friend of hers on mobile and did some chit chat to pass more time. She did not tell her what is going on with her parents as she wanted to keep it a secret till everything normalises. She does not want to take any risk. She then returned home and saw that it is only 11 AM and still more time left to pass as she was expecting a call around 12 PM hoping that by then all the tests and reports would be complete. She then got herself involved with housekeeper in the kitchen and helped her out while having conversation with her. The housekeeper shares how good she is feeling and started crying in front of Sia. This clearly shows what a moment it is for both and for Sia. She has been a long-time loyal housekeeper and has feelings for the family. Even the housekeeper has planned how will she meet and greet her master. She even went to the temple before coming to work and offered prasad to God. She gave the same prasad to Sia and Raghav to have. Both are doing their bit to ensure only positive things happen from now on. They are tired of experiencing problems and issues. They desperately want happiness in their life.

After spending an hour with the housekeeper through helping her out and having deep conversation with her, it was 12PM now and still no sign of phone call. Sia then decided to go for calling the senior doctor on his private mobile number. She has never used this option in the past, but her anxiousness is making her do it. She dialled the doctor. At first, he did not pick up. Sia then put her mobile down and did not ring him again as she feared irritating the senior doctor. However, the doctor was a truly kind person, and he gave a call back to Sia after 5 mins. Sia was Incredibly happy to get a call from him. He asked Sia to wait for a while as reports for last few tests are still pending post which he will surely give a call. Sia asked how her parents are doing, to which the doctor said they are doing fine, and rest have a look herself once she comes, keeping the suspense alive. Sia wanted to hear a lot more information like they are talking, asking for Sia etc but doctor was a senior citizen plus a man of few words so she could not expect much from him. Feeling both happy (that parents are fine) and disappointed (since she did not get any details) she disconnected the call. Even the housekeeper asked curiously what the doctor said, Sia told her everything and even she was disappointed.

Their wait continued for longer than expected. They switched on the television and started watching some music channel to listen to songs and feel better. It is already 2 pm now and they are tired of waiting and getting furious. It is at this moment the phone rings and doctor ask them to come to hospital now. All their frustration and anger changed to excitement. They immediately left for hospital as everything was ready from their side. As soon as the door of the room came where her parents were, Sia asked housekeeper to go inside first along with Raghav, while she took a minute to gather herself and then entered.

OMG! There she saw her parents both father and mother resting in a reclined position with their eyes open as if they were searching for Sia. There were several doctors and nurses standing in the small room so she could not see much from the door. She then moved further inside towards the senior doctor. He signalled to Sia not to cry and control her emotions and behave normally. They cannot take unnecessary stress right now, not good for their health. She then went and stood beside the doctor. So now she could see both clearly. Upon getting a glimpse of Sia, a smile came to her parents face and few drops of tears started pouring out of their eyes. In a feeble voice they both said "Sia beta" at the same time. Doctor tried to pacify them and asked Sia not to cry and gradually take her hands towards them and touch then gently so that they can feel her. They both felt extremely pleasant on getting a feel of Sia. So far so good. Doctor was happy with the way it was going. Sia took permission from doctor to show Raghav to them and then make Raghav also touch their hands one by one. They were so happy to see their son and tears started flowing out again. Doctor then advised Sia to go and sit on the small cot at the side and continue behaving normally. He did not want to give more emotional strain to them. This much was enough. It evaluated also that they are doing fine and remember their family members. They then left the room letting Sia and others spend some time with strict instructions not to talk much and just sit and observe. Once everyone left, Sia just stared at her parents feeling super happy from inside that their eyes are open, and they are reacting to things. It was so surreal for her. All the stress is gone now. All the scenarios that she made in the night nothing worked because now she did what the doctor asked. All her planning went in vain. But its fine. She did not bother much. She was happy and so was the old housekeeper. She also went and stood in front of them and Sia's parents nodded to give the signal that they recognised her. They then just sat there without uttering a single word and just staring at each other and feeling happy about it. What a unique moment. There is so much to talk about, so much to tell, so much has happened but there is complete silence in the room, waiting for the right moment to talk.

Doctor then called Sia and others to his chamber and gave her an update about her parent's health. Doctor said that all the reports are fine, and they do not see any abnormalities. They further mentioned that her parents should start doing activities like talking and walking very soon as they gain more energy and consciousness. He then asked Sia to leave for the day and let them rest. Sia then asked the doctor to see her parents one more time and then she will leave. Doctor agreed. Sia and others went and met them once again touched their hands and gestured that they are leaving for now and will come back very soon. They then left feeling all jovial. There is no stress now. Everything is fine. They just must wait for their health to become better gradually day by day. In a few days they will be discharged, and the entire family will be together at home. What a journey it has been. Full of roller coaster rides. This is what life is. Learn to live every moment in the present as you never know what might happen next.

For a week, Sia used to visit her parents daily sometimes with Raghav sometimes alone. Each day she could see slight progress in their health. Then after a weeks' time, doctor said they will be discharging them tomorrow. So Sia did all the paperwork and made the final payment. She then came the next day along with housekeeper and Raghav to take them home. The hospital arranged an ambulance to drop them at home. The ambulance reached their residence, and the door of the ambulance opened. Madhav and Radha (Sia's parents) looked at their house after so long, felt emotional along with a hint of smile on their face and came out of the ambulance. They then bent down slightly and touched the main gate with their head as a sign of respect to their home. They then slowly moved inside the house. The moment has arrived. They have returned home. Everyone must bid farewell to this world and leave one day but their time has still not come, and they are here to stay for some more time.

Within few months, they started living normal lives. They are now coming back to their original self. Madhav has started doing office work but from home only as of now. Radha has started managing the house slowly.

Sia has now rejoined school in the new session along with Raghav. They both go to the same school. Sia is obviously behind by few years from her friends, but she does not care anymore. She is happy that her parents are back and that she can go to school again and finish her education. She has a new dream now to become a neurologist as she wanted to do more research in this field of neurology and try to find solutions for coma. She wanted to create an impact so that others do not have to go through what she had to.

Raghav is enjoying his nursery school of 3 hours. He initially cried a lot but then got adjusted. At home, Raghav recognised his parents easily and started going to them instantly. Kids can feel their parents no matter how much time gap is there. Also, Sia has made efforts in the past to introduce them to Raghav via their photograph. But he does not call Sia sis or Didi or di. He calls his father "Papa", his mother "Ma" and Sia...

... "CHOTI MAA"!

Chapter 7

What She Lost and What She Got

After this unimaginable journey of last 3 years, Sia is taking a breather now that her parents have taken full control and are back to normal. A big question here is what all did Sia gain and lose in this battle of life. It is important to reflect on the past 3 years with an idea to take a lesson from them and keep that lesson with her for lifetime. The Divine wanted to teach Sia something. Something that was essential and that will give her life the right path. Let us try to review in summary what all did Sia lost and gained. Let us try to understand the crux of it all and if possible, implement in our lives as well.

Losses

1. **Lost her anger** – Sia was very quick in getting irritated. She was short tempered and lost her

cool quickly. This trait spoiled her relationship with her parents' big time. They never said anything to her apart from calming her down, but they were extremely disappointed with her anger. Initially they did try to teach her to maintain cool, but she did not listen. So eventually they stopped teaching her. May be God saw all of this and then he took the reins in his hand and taught Sia a lesson in his own way. As a result, she lost all her anger. She is now a calm person with the ability to understand things better.

2. **Lost her arrogance** – Sia and arrogance were synonyms. She used to show arrogance all the time whether it is her parents or friends. She was full of attitude. Even her friends did not like this about her but still ignored it for the sake of friendship. She did not do any single work at home and never obeyed any instructions from parents. She just did what she liked.

    What God did was he took all those people away from her to teach her a lesson. Her parents went in coma and due to parenting she was cut off from friends. She was alone and all by herself. It was then she realised that her arrogance is unnecessary and troubles the other person. One should be humble and caring.

3.	**Lost her greediness** – Before all of this, it was all about Sia. Every time she thought about herself only. She always thought about what she wants. And her wants never ended. One after the other her new demands arose endlessly. Parents were fulfilling them out of affection which added more fuel to fire. Whenever there was a new phone launched, she wanted that even if she bought a new phone recently. She travelled by car and driver. She wore expensive dresses. Still, she wanted more.

	Then life took a turn for Sia, and it was all about Raghav's demands. Fulfil all the needs of the child she forgot about hers. She then realised that a smile from Raghav gave her more satisfaction than these expensive possessions she once died for. When her parents were in coma all that she wanted was her parents back and was ready to give all her belongings for that. That is the ultimate realisation which killed her greediness forever.

4.	**Reduced attachment** – Parents going into coma was a big setback for Sia. It completely shook her. It took her couple of years to adjust that too partially. After couple of years, she convinced herself that her parents will never return, and she will live like this forever. Keep herself going and avoid the thought of parents she pretended to detach herself from parents. She functioned as if her parents did not mean anything to her. She was faking it. Just to accumulate some strength to face the tough life ahead. In her heart she loved her dearly. It was then she got introduced to the concept of detachment. She tried to reduce her affection and attachment towards her parents in her mind. She was artificially training her mind to do that. Although she was not able to achieve it, but it did help temporarily to live life without parents.

5. **Lost her desires** – All kinds of teenage attraction towards opposite gender in school took a backseat. Earlier she was actively involved in all such things like flirting and talking such stuff with friends. With this sudden burden of responsibility, her mind got totally diverted from all of this. It never came to her mind even once ever since her parents went into coma. Post their return, she completely lost interest in all of this after living the life of a parent.

Gains

1. **Calm and polite** – After a lot of struggles of parenting, Sia realized that one thing which is not working at all is irritation and anger. It makes the situation worse and the child cries even more. The only way out is to keep calm, have politeness and behave softly with kid. With multiple such iterations, it became Sia's habit. It has now become a part of her natural personality.

2. **Giving nature** – With only giving and caring for the child for so many months without being able to think about oneself there are high chances that one will become a giver. Sia did not have time to even comb her hair which is the case with most of the moms. Not being able to take out time for herself and fulfilling the needs of the child made her a natural giver just like a mother. She completely stopped thinking about herself and all she thought was about Raghav. Even when one of her friends casually visited Sia's place to meet her, she was shocked to see how Sia was asking her to eat and drink and brought several items for her to have just like elderly ladies do at home. All the time she insisted her friend to have one more snack. She was never like this. The thought that the other person might be

thirsty or hungry never came to her mind earlier. This shows she has become a giver now.

3.   **Hardworking & responsible** – Sia who was so lazy and who never followed a single instruction of her parent can never be seen resting now. She is always doing something. She does not like sitting idle now. Either she is looking after the kid, arranging the house, or cooking or planning for the coming days. She is always busy. This also helped her to avoid the thought of missing her parents. Now she has started liking it this way. It has become ingrained in her nature.

4.   **Emotional** – One thing which she has developed is difficult to categorise as a gain or a loss. It is both. She has become emotional and sensitive. After facing so much in life that too abruptly anyone is bound to become like that. She now cries very easily on small issues. She panics fast. Even a small movie scene can bring tears to her eyes. A part of it is because she can now feel the pain of the other person. She has become empathetic. Feeling others pain and working towards resolving it is fine and a welcome change but getting moved by it so much and let it affect your own mental health is problematic. May be gradually she can learn to keep that distinction.

With the kind of progress, she has shown till now, she can make it possible.

5. **Humble** – All the arrogance she had, has faded away. Earlier everything was about Sia. But now no more self-pompousness. She gives due importance and respect to everyone around her. She does not glorify her achievements and maintains silence. Earlier she used to blabber a lot about her possessions or small achievements. But now she loves to work in the background and let the work do the talking.

6. **Started valuing things** – She was extremely careless and reckless earlier. She did not have the sense to meticulously keep even her most valuable possession. She used to throw her costly wristwatch on the bed or table, forget her pricy mobile every time everywhere. She has already lost lot of her original gold earrings. But she never cared and never felt sad about it thinking Papa will buy another one for her. Now when she saw Raghav doing the exact same thing, she got furious. Raghav did it purely because he is just a small child who does not know the value, however Sia did it even after knowing the value. When Raghav broke a few costly show pieces kept in the living room which Sia only bought for her father, Sia got an eyeopener on how it feels

to lose something costly and precious. She then developed a feeling of sensitivity towards all the material possessions and started caring for them ensuring their long life.

No guidance or moral support

Doing physical labour and having lot of work to finish is one kind of stress, however primary stress comes when there is no guidance from senior or moral support. This is when one must take a decision on their own and face the consequences. If anyone experienced person is at home then, one can get expert advice and taking decision becomes a lot easier. One feels comfortable that an experienced and senior person has blessed the decision so it will give the right results.

In Sia's case there was no comfort. She was the sole decision maker and did not have any clue at the start whether she is making the right choice or not. From a small decision like which milk bottle to buy, which diaper to use, what oil to apply for massage to decide which dal will be better for child's digestion, she had only the old housekeeper to talk to. But the final authority was Sia only. So, she was always confused, the housekeeper did try to give assurance, but a parent's assurance is something else. Although the housekeeper was experienced but she followed several old traditions in managing a child which are no longer used in parenting. So Sia could not blindly trust her suggestion. She had to apply her own mind and do her own research. If parents were there at home, but assuming they were not able to do any work, still it would have been one thousand times easier as only their mere presence and their verbal instructions were enough. That is the impact a parent has. They are like the roof of a house. If they are not there, then you are left with no roof. Then all the sun, rain and winter will start entering the house and you must face it.

Every time that subtle feeling remains in mind and heart, of what dad or mom would have done in such a situation. This feeling is a constant. Even 30–40-year-old adults feel it when they lose their parents. The child tends to imitate his or her parents when they lose them. My dad or mom used to do like this so I will also do it. They take pride in it. Such is the impact of parents in the mind of their children which they only realize after their parents are gone.